KREMLIN KILLING GROUND

As Col. Dean Sturgis and Zandark moved through the narrow underground tunnel, they thought they were unseen. But eyes watched through a hole in the stone walls; twin blue beacons of hate. Glassnose was pleased to have these two new subjects enter his domain.

The Kremlin torturer rushed along the parallel passageway and exited ahead of the intruders into the corridor. He raised his huge three-inch barreled weapon and fired.

Sturgis heard a pop and saw a shell hit the floor beneath his feet. Then it burst open, releasing a dense cloud of white choking smoke.

"Gas!" the colonel yelled. "Let's . . ."

But suddenly he couldn't speak or breathe. He blacked out before he hit the stone floor.

C.A.D.S.

#6 TECH INFERNO

JOHN SIEVERT

ZEBRA BOOKS
KENSINGTON PUBLISHING CORP.

ZEBRA BOOKS

are published by

Kensington Publishing Corp.
475 Park Avenue South
New York, NY 10016

First printing: July, 1988

Printed in the United States of America

FORWARD

World War III, which the U.S. lost, left much of the world a radioactive hell. The victorious Soviets landed on the east coast of America but were not able to move beyond the Appalachian Mountains—due to the efforts of the ragtag American Resistance and the awesome C.A.D.S commandos, led by Col. Dean Sturgis.

C.A.D.S. headquarters was at the underground White Sands, New Mexico base, also the new home of the Wartime White House, headed by President Williamson.

Colonel Sturgis was the commander of the president's special force of two hundred high-tech soldiers who wore the multimillion dollar Computerized Attack and Defense Suit. C.A.D.S. battle gear was a spacesuitlike armored outfit equipped with a plethora of deadly armaments. Never had the world known such weapons! Each magna-steel and plastisynth C.A.D.S. suit had the firepower of a whole battalion of regular soldiers—everything from flamethrowers to "E-balls"—deadly electro-charged high-explosive shells. All the weapons were computer targeted and fired through a "weapons tube" below the C.A.D.S. warrior's right arm. All a C.A.D.S. trooper had to do was point and fire!

The C.A.D.S. suits were a high-tech wonder, but due to the unavailability of many parts, many substitutions and shortcuts have been made in them. This had diminished their function—more push was required on the servo-mechanism power-assists by human muscles. Now the jet-packs had limited range; the underwater capabilities were completely nullified by seal-substitutions in the five years since the war. But there had been adaptations that *enhanced* the suits as well: For instance, the V.S.R.—Variable Shell-Fire system. This adaptation allowed a soldier to use captured ammo in his firing system—no matter what caliber.

The C.A.D.S. unit rode three-wheel high-powered motorcycles, called Tri-wheelers; Tris for short. The Tris once ran on fuel cell power, but now, five years after *N-day,* the motorcycles had been adapted to function on waste oil or gasoline.

The inner circle of C.A.D.S. officers, six men and one woman, led all the missions. They were all veteran fighters of post-war America; all had fought many times against the Soviet might, and survived.

First and foremost among them was Col. Dean Sturgis, a.k.a. "the Tech Commando." Over six feet tall, he had sandy blond hair, brown eyes. He held a vast knowledge of the C.A.D.S. suit and its capabilities. Sturgis was once an astronaut trainee, but was canned for insubordination when he questioned safety problems on the Shuttle mission. His nature was rebellious and he was contemptuous of bureaucrats. His obsession was to once again be with his wife, Robin Adler, who was somewhere out there in war-ravaged America.

Fenton MacLeish, the British C.A.D.S. trooper, was a member of the Queen's elite Black Guard. He was sent to the U.S. in 1996 for training in use of the C.A.D.S. suit. He stayed when World War III suddenly broke out. He became more than an ally; he became an integral member of the C.A.D.S. unit.

Billy (the Kid) Dixon, height five feet ten, platinum-blond hair, husky with shoulders like a table, was indispensable on all missions. A crazed Audie Murphy type of bravery characterized his actions against the Soviets. The Southerner was the first over the barriers in any action.

Mickey Rossiter was the technical expert and mechanic of the unit. Once overweight and clumsy, the exigencies of post-nuke warfare made him lean and hard—and careful. A master tinker, he could fix things without the proper tools or parts. And often he had to do just that.

Tranh Van Noc was a Vietnamese American. He had served with Sturgis in Southeast Asia, in the post-Vietnam rescue of M.I.A.s. The mystic of the group, Tranh preferred to remain silent when he could be.

Dr. Sheila DeCamp was one of the few women trained in "driving" the C.A.D.S. suit. Often this tall and spunky medical doctor with a degree in psychoanalysis was argumentative with Sturgis. But secretly she loved him. Sheila was attractive, with shoulder-length chestnut hair.

Joe Fireheels was the most recent member added to the group. He came from the Four Corners area of Arizona. A full-blooded American Indian, Fireheels was adept at infiltration. He seemed to have a sixth sense for survival. He replaced Roberto Fuentes, who died in the service of his country a year earlier, but lived on in the C.A.D.S. troopers' cherished memories.

These officers and their metal-clad soldiers of destiny were the only force capable of stopping the Soviets from totally overwhelming America.

CHAPTER 1

The skies over New City, Oregon, a small farming community, were clear and blue for the first time since the Nuke War; the summer wheat waving in the autumn fields was healthy and tall. On a hill overlooking the peaceful scene was a gray-bearded man in a bent and dirty stovepipe hat. His name was Hendricks, and his steely gray eyes surrounded by deep wrinkles had seen much much worse in the past few years. As a matter of fact, he thought, it was just about the *prettiest* scene, on the *prettiest* day, that Hendricks could remember. True, he only remembered the days since the war—before that was a blank. Concussion, they said. So American history started with Christmas Eve, 1997, when the bombs fell.

He had lost his wife then, rest her soul, but he only knew that because *they* told him so. The five years since the "blowup," as they called it locally, had seen three-quarters of the U.S. population die. Forty million or so died outright that hell-mushroom night, three times that many since. Most initial survivors had succumbed to rad-sickness, plague, or plain old-fashioned starvation. And another twenty-five million fell victims to their own countrymen, fighting for what was left of the supplies of food, water, and shelter.

But today was five years later and far better times. Hendricks had a new wife, two surviving strong children—the first one born had died by Hendricks' own hands in its first day of life. Hendricks had killed the lobsterlike boy-creature himself with the butt of his rifle. But the other two, a boy and a girl, grew up all right. And now there were crops—and even meat to eat. He had the ferrets—good meat source—romping in the pen behind the white-painted clapboard house. The first ferrets had been a gift of the U.S. emergency government men who had come by last year. "God bless President Williamson," Hendricks mumbled, "for now hope abounds!"

Now it was sunny and bright and beautiful and the crops were all right and the fledgling survival town had farming and husbandry, and even a church! By gum, this here part of Oregon had its act together, by God it did!

Hendricks turned to see his boy Joss coming up the hill, all fifty-eight cowlicked pounds of him. The boy waved excitedly.

"Pa—you gotta see the new ferrets—one's got three eyes! I swear!"

"Never mind 'bout those new ferrets son, jes' stand here—Jes' look at that wheat waving, Joss." He pulled on his boy's sleeve. The pale blue-eyed boy said, "Aw Pop, it always looks like that!"

10

"No son, it's brighter today. The sky is brighter and bluer than ever and so's the wheat—just look at her roll!"

Then his expression changed. For he perceived a line crawling across the sky—a black line in a blue sky. And as he watched, the line broke up and branched. It looked strange, and yet familiar. What was it about those lines!

Yes! It was just like the thing he had seen against the face of the winter moon that night—in December—the last night of the old world. The night of death that had wiped his previous forty years of life from his mind, like chalk is wiped off a slate.

The word *MIRV* came into his mind. What did it mean? His heart pounded—it meant—*death*. Hendricks had to do something—what?

He had to get the family into the storm cellar, the one he built to protect them from the mega-storms. Whatever MIRV was had something to do with nukes. Bad stuff. Death-stuff.

Suddenly his lips became dry. MIRV meant Multiwarhead Independent Reentry Vehicle. *Nuclear Missiles*. He turned back toward the house, yanking his son by the arm. He yelled, "Jenny! Jenny! Where's Jenny?" The three-year-old girl came out on the porch wiping her hands on her homespun apron. And right behind her came a sturdy, freckled country-type woman—the picture of an ideal wife; Mary was that.

"What is it dear?"

"In the sky!" Hendricks shouted.

As Hendricks lifted the protesting Joss into his arms he glanced over his shoulder. One of the black

11

lines was coming *down,* right at New City.

Jenny caught and followed his look.

"Oh God," she exclaimed. "Is it heading for us?"

"Never mind. Get Jenny in the cellar." He pushed her inside the screen door.

"Ow Daddy, hey why so rough?" Joss protested as Hendricks dropped him on the old carpet.

"Just get in the hole in that cellar, son—and be brave. Take your baby sister."

"Why can't I stay out? Aren't we gonna play baseball?"

"Later—*get down there!*"

Hendricks' wife protested. "But ain't you coming?"

The man stood tall. "No, I ain't—just yet. You shut the door. Do it!"

He had never spoken to her so harshly. So Mary did as he demanded. Hendricks—she never knew his whole name, neither did he—was a good builder. He had built this cellar solid and deep. She had, for an instant as she lit the big candle, a vision in her mind's eye. She saw herself standing there last year, arms akimbo, criticizing him. "Hendricks! Why so deep? Why so solid? We just need a root cellar, that's all. A place to store the jars of preserves and such. Why, if you take too long, Hendricks, the winter will be here before the cellar even—"

"Just a little deeper," he had said. And Hendricks had worked with his big hands and hairy strong arms until the frost came, and he finished the cellar. They near froze that winter so's this cellar could be so deep and strong. But now, it could save them. Mary knew that another N-day had come though he

12

never had said what the sky-streak meant. She held the two children close to her. "Please God," she muttered. *"Please!"*

"Momma," Jenny protested, "why can't Daddy come down now—even with the candle it's so dark. Why are we down here?" The little girl began to sob.

"Shhh, it's a game. Just a game . . ." She wept silently, biting her lips, trying to control her voice when she said, "Children, we stay down here and hide for a long time, and then we go up. That's the game."

Hendricks, cursing under his breath at every commie bastard that ever was, loaded up his big blunderbuss and walked out on the porch. Funny, he *remembered* his old life now. Remembered a wife, two kids, just like now; remembered his salesman days—a route from Canada to Arizona. He remembered most proudly that he had been a soldier, serving his country. His heart swelled with pride. Yes—he had stood up to America's enemies before—and he'd do it again now.

Hendricks muttered, "Don't know if it'll work, but I gotta try. I'm gonna try and shoot the damned thing down—'fore it hits." He'd do it for his old life, for his great country that had been smashed down. It was time to stand up to the Russkies—or die trying!

Hendricks stood on the porch and watched the gleaming dot in front of the black smoke trail. It was a *warhead,* falling attached to a red parachute. Just a heavy silver cannister like a milk pail! Its drop-chute caught in the wind, blowing it his way, slowing it down.

By golly, maybe it *is* close enough . . .

Hendricks watched it rock back and forth, coming closer and closer. It was quite pretty actually, this gleaming head of death glinting in the sun. It had a little yellow hammer and sickle on its shiny metal surface. It was that close!

He lifted his rifle, sighted, and gave a little extra height for distance. Then he fired at it, emptied the gun at the death thing.

There was one *ping*. Hendricks smiled, exclaimed, "Got it!"

His eyeballs vaporized in the first flash of the nuclear air-burst explosion one hundred yards away. Gamma, alpha, and beta rays rode on a million degrees expanding ball of heat, making Hendricks and his house into a powdery gray shadow on the suddenly blackened soil.

The fireball grew like a red cancer on the tan surface of the western fields, consuming everything in its expanding domain. Everywhere on the surface, the very cells of trees, animals, and humans, in one micro-instant, were incinerated, evaporated, turned to gasses. Anything within a mile of ground zero.

As for Hendricks's family, they were not so lucky. The mother's and children's clothing burst into flames. Screaming their death screams, they beat at their burning garments, their skin flaming, breathing steam not air, blood coming out of their ruptured, exploded eyes, their ears, their mouths.

That was just the shock wave. Then the temperature went to 460 degrees, 480 degrees, 500 degrees.

As merciful relief, death came.

Brains expanded and splashed through wide nostrils, and the three sank down on the dirt floor, just a baking black pile of fused skin and bones, looking like an irregular-shaped bun left in the oven too long.

A half mile away, a couple crossing a tarred street in the twelve-house center of town were forever etched onto the black of the pavement. They had just evaporated, their shadows made into a silhouette picture.

A woman standing by a window was suddenly just a hot skeleton with flaming hair. The hair, no longer held by flesh, sprayed off and stuck to the far wall, over the salvaged picture of Whistler's mother.

A mile away, a man in a jeep—the town's mayor—was thrown with his vehicle for a hundred yards. He flew right through Elmo's barn wall. Then, screaming, aflame, the gray-haired gent steered the jeep wildly among the burning boards and chickens in a wild circle, until he slumped over the melting wheel. The jeep's gas tank exploded, finishing off the burning barn.

By far, the lucky ones were the ones like Hendricks who were there one second, and just simply weren't the next.

Yet it was a small explosion by nuclear standards. A hundred kilotons, a mini-bomb, smaller than the first bomb ever dropped on people—the Hiroshima bomb. But it did its job. The sky so blue was lit up, so that farmers in faraway fields, way over the rolling hills, had to shield their eyes and look away. Even then, they could see the bones in their hands clearly through their closed eyelids. The retina-burning white flash of the small warhead of an intercontinental ballistic missile—one of three warheads of the MIRV—had done its job. This gleaming cannister had taken out New City. The other two warheads fell 136 and 321 miles away, destroying Oak Dale Settlement and the Utah Airdrome; destroying places built of dreams and longings and hope. Destroying hope above all things.

The survivors of those disasters crawled on the ground and wept, and gnashed their teeth for their lost loved ones, for their lost dream of peace and normalcy. And their one anguished cry was: When would it ever end?

The survival settlement of New City was a mass of swirling flaming boards and melting metal girders. The fireball expanded, and its hell-gasses of a million degree temperature cooled. The fireball became a climbing mushroom-shaped cloud, slowly rising to 100,000 feet high. The shock wave, moving at 700 miles per hour, expanded from it in concentric lines; it smashed down what had not been evaporated into primeval atoms by the initial blast.

Death ruled.

CHAPTER 2

From the air, the sandy surface looked like any other part of the southwestern desert of the United States: some rolling dunes, twisted cacti, boulders scattered in a tumble, a few jagged rock outcroppings.

But it wasn't like any other place on earth. Below the faceless ground was the new United States White House, and a vast multileveled city of factories and living quarters inhabited by over 10,000 people. White Sands Base.

As the purple sun flickered over the eastern horizon half lost in strontium haze left over from the Nuke War 3,300 men slept, and 6,600 worked. Much of the work was military—armaments manufacture. And the most intricate, desperate work was on the huge Level 7 Armor-suit Production unit. There, technicians and skilled weapons-artisans assembled the marvels called the C.A.D.S. suits. The workers struggled, making compromises on the design of these armor-fighting suits, because there were no

17

places outside this facility to provide needed high-tech parts. They knew they had to work harder, faster, *smarter,* for without C.A.D.S. suits and the men that wore them—no U.S.A. at all.

The C.A.D.S. warriors' leader, a man known as The Tech Commando, Colonel Sturgis, was still having a sound sleep, in the arms of a gentle, beautiful woman. There was not a sound, not a light at his Level 5 compartment, one of the twenty levels of a complex expanded after the war from the original base called Omega Command. Sturgis, for the first time in weeks, had no nightmarish dreams. There was just a sleepy comfort, felt somehow through the sense beyond consciousness. Safe. Warm. Loved.

And beautiful, hot-house frail Morgana, her dark hair spilled over the white pillow, felt the same warmth and security in the arms of this man of all men.

Then came loud repeated knocks on the oak door that sent Sturgis bolt upright. He automatically lifted his right arm, turned his fingers in the direction of the noise, as if he were in his C.A.D.S. suit, and said, "Fire!"

When he heard no shot, he understood where he was. And exhaled the tension.

He hit the light switch and Morgana pulled the sheets up over her pear-shaped breasts. Sturgis yelled, "Okay, okay, stop banging!" He pulled on his shorts and went to the door, opened it a crack.

"What the *hell* is it?" He glanced at the crisply dressed MP and then at the luminous-dial clock on the dresser. "Do you know what time it is, soldier?"

18

"Five A.M. sir! But there's a call from the president himself for you. You must have your phone accidentally off the hook, sir, so it was sent from the guard station and . . ."

"Right!" Sturgis said. God, why did President Williamson want him at this hour? He opened the door. The MP was familiar to Sturgis. "Okay, Remsen . . . Sorry." He tried to smile. "I'm sorry for the peeve—what did the president say?"

"Sir, there's an extraordinary session of the War Cabinet convening in twenty minutes. They want you there, sir." Remsen saluted sharply.

"Okay," Sturgis said. "Hold on. Let me dress. Then you've got to lead me through this damned maze. The base expands and changes every day. I could get lost."

As Sturgis put on his clothes, Morgana got up, naked. She walked to him, pushed back her hair and kissed him. "Luck," she said.

He wanted to stay but he nodded. "I'll need it."

In a minute, he strode forcefully down the long snaking corridors behind Remsen. They went to an elevator, went down two levels. The elevator door opened to incessant hammering. Construction was going on even at this hour, hardening, deepening the White Sands, New Mexico complex. The base was two miles square now and getting bigger—on a longitudinal north-south axis. All underground.

They found the new elevator bank. "This area wasn't here two days ago," Remsen stated proudly. They got in the shiny car and, riding down two more levels, came out into another corridor, one with wide mahogany doors at its end. A pair of guards opened the doors, and Sturgis walked alone into a circular, wood-paneled room. It smelled musky.

The president and his four inner confidants, seated at a long, raised mahogany counter, looked up from a vid-screen display they were watching. Seated immediately to the right of the tall, lanky Oklahoman president was Admiral Turner. The colonel noticed the wooly-eyebrowed hothead hadn't bothered to comb his mass of unruly dark hair.

Turner sneered at Sturgis, whose keen brown eyes merely passed to the man next to him, Science Advisor Sidney Gridley. The arthritic, sixty-year-old gray-haired Gridley had his knobby cane on the table before him, as if ready to strike with it. His wildly tousled hair seemed more disheveled than ever. To the left of the president was a large-bodied, tall, gaunt, man of power, C.I.A. Director Stanford Quartermain, busy shuffling his pile of briefing papers. To the C.I.A. man's right was the bristle-crewcut red-haired General Burns, chomping on his unlit panatella cigar.

Sturgis frowned. All of them except the president, had, at one time or another, tried to "do in" Sturgis, by court-martial, reassignment, or demotion—and failed. Sturgis didn't think much of this *rump* War Cabinet at all. Why were these men Sturgis called the "Acid Four" the ultimate advisors to the president? Politics was a strange and disconcerting thing!

General Knolls, the commander of the base, and Dr. Van Patten, Chief of Research, used to be in on

20

all meetings, and they should still be, Sturgis thought. Gradually, the free U.S. government was becoming rule-by-quintet. Sturgis especially loathed "Nuke-'em-Now" Turner. Why an admiral should be in this holy of holies setting defied imagination. There was, after all, no more navy! But the colonel kept those thoughts to himself.

"Good of you to come," President Williamson said, opening the meeting. "I know it's your sleep period and—"

"What's up?" asked Sturgis, slipping into one of the seats arranged in front of the five men. He stared at Williamson, at the man he had almost shot a year earlier. The president was getting prematurely gray, and no wonder, given the job, given his advisors. Sturgis realized that he had aged a lot himself—they all had. War, constant, grinding war, does that to you.

"Look at this readout from scan-command," the president said, turning the vid-screen console for Sturgis to see.

Sturgis saw what he meant. "Three survival towns are off-line?"

"Worse than that, colonel! Air-recon confirms multiple hits by nuke warheads—small-kiloton jobs—have taken out two towns. *Plus* our Utah air base—the home of our only paradrop command. All six C-47's are destroyed. The base, before it was hit, got a read on an approaching ICBM. It was coming on a trajectory from the Soviet Union."

"Confirmed?"

"Confirmed, colonel," the president said grimly.

Sturgis sat back. "But how could they do that?

The world is radioactive enough, *isn't it?* These targets are really very minor! Don't they realize—"

"Evidently the Reds thought hitting at us is more important than a little more radiation! The weather was calm, the fallout will not be too bad by the time it reaches Russia."

"Any lines on how the Reds knew of those three targets?"

"Negative," Martel said. Sturgis turned to see that the impish Brian Martel, his black curly hair showing signs of needing a trim, had just entered the chamber. The young electronics genius sat down next to Sturgis, smiling and winking—a welcome warm presence among this bunch of hanging-judge types, Sturgis thought. "The Reds still don't have a functioning satellite camera," Martel continued. "There were no overflights by them of the areas. I suspect it was just word-of-mouth. Careless lips, or spies tipped the Soviets off. Maybe some biker gang got a glimpse of the towns, sold the info in the East."

"Yes," Turner snapped, pointing his finger at Martel. "But only because you've failed us, Martel. You're in charge of intercepting Soviet communications. Why didn't you tell us what they were up to, sonny?"

Martel turned beet red, stuttered out, "Sir! If it was discussed on the air waves anywhere in a thousand miles of here, or even on shortwave lengths further away, I would have recorded it and decoded it!"

Burns spoke up. "That's not the issue—the issue is: Now what do we do about it?"

Turner, shaking with acerbic rage, said, as Sturgis expected, "Nuke 'em back!"

The admiral turned his shaking finger toward Sturgis. "In any case, colonel, this is a whole new phase of the war." Turner glared at Sturgis as if *he* had done it, as if it was the colonel's fault the towns were nuked. "We shouldn't spend so much time and effort on your C.A.D.S. commandos; we should concentrate on building a few big bombers, getting together some nukes—and get them back! What do you say?"

Sturgis replied dryly, "If we did bomb the Soviets again, it would increase the radiation here in the U.S.A., too."

"But we can't keep getting *hit* like this," Gridley chimed in.

Sturgis said, "What do you think, General Burns? You're unusually silent . . ."

The bristle-crewcut redhead snapped. "Just thinking. Thinking of strangling that bastard, Premier Belyakov!"

The president addressed Sturgis. "Dean, you know what the loss of Utah Airdrome means?"

"Yes. No more paradrops of the C.A.D.S. unit in the East. But we'll go overland. We did it before. We will keep hitting the Reds in the East anyway, drive them off into the sea."

"Can't do that anymore," said C.I.A. Director Quartermain. "They've got new air surveillance units to stop overland attacks now. They'd spot your unit at the Mississippi. Bomb the hell out of you and your men. No, Sturgis, the C.A.D.S. unit, with the loss of the C-47 airdrop planes, has lost its effectiveness."

"If it ever had any," Turner cut in, fuming mad. "Might as well disband C.A.D.S. now!"

"That's not the only planes we have," Sturgis shouted. "How about the Hercules in Arizona? A big four-engine job—long range; they can airlift my men East!"

"How the hell," interjected Quartermain, "did you know about the Hercules, colonel? That's top secret!"

Sturgis didn't let on that Martel had told him. Instead, the colonel replied enigmatically, "You can't keep secrets from me."

Martel, the foremost electronic wizard in the whole damned world—with a specialty in eavesdropping devices—looked down and smirked. He and Sturgis were allies against the establishment.

Sturgis continued. "Anyway, I can use that Hercules plane for our next C.A.D.S. attack East."

"No," said Williamson. "I believe the time is past for commando attacks. We have to come up with something to directly affect the ability of the Reds to launch nukes at us."

"Get the Herc outfitted to carry those nuke warheads we found in the silo in Kansas," Turner said. "Fly right into the Goddamned Soviet Union and let 'em have one more dose of—"

"All that would happen," said Sturgis, "is that the Hercules would be shot down." He drummed the chair arm in impatience.

"Right, their radar is still up," Martel added. "I

verfied that electronically."

"What about your Intelligence Unit, Quartermain?" asked the president. "What do you know of the Red air defense?"

"Formidable," Quartermain admitted. "The Herc wouldn't get in."

Sturgis spoke up. "I think others should now be called in on this meeting. We need more imput to make these crucial decisions. How about General Knolls and Van Patten? Van Patten's research and development, and Knolls is, you know, still in charge of this base."

The president looked around. One by one the four advisors shook their heads no. The president turned to Sturgis.

"Dean, this has to remain among us few. It will cause a panic if word of the nukings gets out. We have six thousand refugees here—they're difficult enough to handle and keep busy at productive tasks. We want to keep this meeting, and what it's about, under wraps. Several ideas have been raised here. But I need more ideas. I want to adjourn this meeting now. You all know the problem. I want clever solutions, gentlemen. Plans for victory. We meet back here tomorrow at thirteen hundred hours; and you all come up with something new to stop the nukings!"

Sturgis sneered at each and every one of them—except the president—as he rose to leave with Martel. "We have to ask Van Patten and Knolls," Sturgis whispered as they left the room. "They're not blabbermouths. You want to help me to come up with a new plan, Martel?"

The young man nodded. "We surely can come up with something better than counter-nuking! These guys have all been underground too long. Only the president ever goes topside! They're like mad rats, colonel."

"Don't I know it."

CHAPTER 3

Sturgis called a secret breakfast meeting in the officer's cafeteria on Level 2. Sturgis arrived first, put two quarters in the coffee machine and got his black coffee. A half cup later Brian Martel arrived. "Close the door," Sturgis said. "Got the stuff?"

Martel nodded, put a black satchel down on the formica-top table and opened it. He quickly set up his electro-scan for bugs and his black box blackout-wave-creator. When that gadget was lit up, Martel smiled. "We can talk now—there are bugs here, like we expected, but my device will neutralize them. No one listening in will hear a word; no sound leaves this area. Beyond a circle of ten feet there's no sound or visual image—we're just a black hole in space!"

Knolls and Van Patten arrived and sat down. The white-haired distinguished-looking general put on his pince-nez glasses and looked at the papers Sturgis had laid out, one for each man. Van Patten lit and sucked on his meerschaum pipe, staring at the winking red light on Martel's black box. "We're going to get in trouble for this meeting," Van

Patten said.

"No one can hear a thing we say in here, thanks to Martel," Sturgis said. He explained about Martel's devices.

"Amazing," Van Patten uttered. Martel winked. "A cinch!"

Sturgis wondered if the young genius they all called the New Edison wasn't putting them on this time with the blackout device! But he had done amazing things before: reactivated a communications satellite from the White Sands radio station;* invented a device that protected anyone from killer-microwave transmission without armor; plus a dozen other minor and major miracles of science. Sturgis filled Knolls and Van Patten in on the situation regarding the three nuked targets—plus the cabinet meeting they had missed.

"Well," said Knolls, "I can't imagine a way to counter-blow the Reds—how about you, Martel? Maybe you can start us off."

Everyone looked at Martel. The young man shrugged. "We can't zap Russia from here—we have no missiles. And they probably have a hundred active ABMs to protect their launch sites anyway. I pass."

Van Patten put down his pipe. "Offhand—I can't add anything. My R and D department has no new projects at all."

Sturgis frowned. "Martel and I were told not to talk about the three nukings. They don't want it to leak out and cause a panic on base. But I need some input. We have to come up with a plan of action to

* See C.A.D.S. #3.

28

counter the threat. I hoped that two more heads would help to come up with a fresh idea. *Come on! Let's brainstorm.* Just say anything that comes to mind—no matter how fantastic."

For the next hour, Sturgis heard many bizarre comments. The serious talk became draining. But then it got to be downright silly, after Martel began adding Scotch to their many coffees.

Knolls smiled, "Drop shit on the premier—from a big bird!"

Van Patten laughed and said, "Yeah, kill the premier with a C.A.D.S. suit—kick! That'll stop them."

Martel said, "Psychically influence Premier Belyakov to commit suicide." He put his head down on the formica, giggling.

Sturgis grabbed Van Patten's shoulder. "That's it—what did you just say?"

"What? I said kill Belyakov, with a C.A.D.S. kick! But we can't—"

"We *can!*" said Sturgis. "We combine Knoll's 'drop shit on him' with your 'kill him.' Listen! What if the Hercules four-engine jet at Arizona Base can get my men to Russia?"

"No," Knolls said. "Radar would pick up the Herc and missiles would shoot it down."

Martel said drunkenly, "It can fly low, land-ho! Drop C.A.D.S. troopers on the ice cap, before it reaches Russia. They can just walk in!"

"*Good!*" Sturgis said. "Very good. That's exactly what we need. We go to the source of the trouble—in Russia—and cut it out, like a cancer. But I only have

29

six operational suits."

Van Patten said, "I can give you some new down-scale C.A.D.S. suits, Sturgis. But what good that will do, I don't know. Even if you get some men into Russia, the premier is in the Kremlin, man! I suggest a less hair-brained plan—we track down the traitors who fingered the targets for the Reds. End of problem. Simple."

"Yeah," replied the colonel, "except we don't have a line on them. Besides, there will be new traitors—security zones are already tight, camouflage is strung everywhere, but men are men . . . and rats—rats! No, short of going there and wringing the neck of the damned premier, I don't think we can stop the attacks. And if we do kill Belyakov, there will be a civil war in Russia. His death will leave a power vacuum."

Knolls stuttered, red-faced. "And whoever is next in charge over there—even if he was a damned rabid Red—wouldn't poison the world anymore with nukes, like that madman Belyakov."

"That's it," said Sturgis.

"What's it?" asked Van Patten amused, and confused.

"We go there. The C.A.D.S. team goes to Russia and kills the premier. Go to the source of the problem in the Kremlin. I'll take ten, maybe twenty C.A.D.S. men and paradrop on the ice, walk into Russia, get to the Kremlin—"

"Hate to throw water on this scheme," said Knolls, "but the Hercules's range isn't good enough for even a flight to Russia's border. And there's no more KC-135 air-tankers for refueling in midair, you know. Plus—well, it's a rather *bizarre . . ."*

Sturgis looked over at Martel. "Can you and Van Patten and engineering form a task force, find a way to modify the Hercules to get more mileage?"

Martel nodded. "With computerized fuel control, computer wind analysis—all of the things that can be done to get more range—yes! We can increase the aircraft's range."

"Plus," said Van Patten excitedly, "some streamlining of the plane to reduce drag! We can use the K-mode variable surface ailerons . . . and . . ."

"It's a crazy idea," Knolls said. Then he smirked, meaning he liked it.

"Can I go along?" Martel begged. "Maybe you, er, need me to monitor electronics onboard. I'm checked out in the C.A.D.S. suit . . ."

Sturgis looked pained, and they all stared at Martel who lowered his eyes. "I know," he said softly. "I'm too valuable to risk. Dammit!"

When Sturgis explained his proposal to the Acid Five cabinet, they were against it. All except Williamson, who said, "I think you have something here, Sturgis. The Reds certainly aren't expecting *this!"*

The Oklahoman turned to Quartermain. "What's the intel on who is next in line to be premier?"

Quartermain dryly said, "What little we know indicates a massive power struggle would occur in the Kremlin if Belyakov died. But—"

Sturgis interrupted. "Mr. President, we can't dictate who will take over if the premier dies—but

31

the next man has got to be less crazy than the man who started World War Three. Agreed?"

"Yeah, all except Veloshnikov," said Gridley. "If he takes over he'll be as bad—"

"I can't believe this!" interjected Turner, red-faced. "I can't believe that you're actually talking about sending men into the Kremlin itself and killing the premier. It's—Goddamned *impossible!*"

There was a moment of shocked silence. "Of course . . ." Williamson said softly, "if it could be done . . . it might save the country . . ."

Sturgis seized the moment. "It *can* be done! It *has* to be done!" he shouted. He rattled off the plan that his team had developed in the cafeteria.

"You have it all worked out?" Burns smiled. "Moscow is thousands of miles into Russia. Once you get into Russia—if you do, how the hell will you remain undetected?"

Sturgis opened his folder marked *Talltree*—his code name for the mission. "I propose that a C.A.D.S. team of twenty men, once paradropped on the icecap off Siberia, will walk to land. The power-assist C.A.D.S. suits can walk ten miles an hour. We *steal* transport—a covered truck maybe—and get more speed that way. We can knock out anything or anyone that tries to stop us with our C.A.D.S. weapons. Once we are in Russia, it's just like any other penetrate-and-destroy mission. We go into the Kremlin and wipe the place out with E-balls and missiles and explosive charges! Make sure we blast the premier!"

"You've thought this out very well," admired the president. "What do you think, gentlemen?" He looked around steely-eyed. The admiral still shook his head, mumbled under his breath words that sounded like "foolishness . . . insane . . ."

"Any *better* ideas?" Williamson asked.

Turner threw up his hands. "No!"

"Okay," Williamson said. "We vote. Raise your hands if you want Sturgis to go ahead."

The vote was three to two, Turner and Burns opposing. The president, Quartermain, and Gridley, smiled.

"Operation Talltree," said Williamson, "is approved!"

CHAPTER 4

Sturgis wanted to get the jet ready and get the mission off the ground within a week. He ordered Martel to send a scramble message to the Arizona base to get the Hercules flight-operational. They sent a team of engineers and welders—everyone needed—to modify the plane according to Martel and Van Patten's ideas. Brian was glad to suit up and get the hell out into the "real world," as he put it. He wouldn't be going to Russia, but Williamson admitted the necessity of sending the "genius of White Sands" to supervise the refitting of the big Hercules.

Sturgis was at the exit ramp to see Martel off. The young man sat in his C.A.D.S. suit atop his idling Tri-bike. He shook hands—carefully—with the colonel and said, "If the Russkies or Pinky Ellis* comes along—" Martel lifted his weapons tube and clicked its empty smg trigger. "I'll waste 'em."

Sturgis smiled. "You do that, Brian. Shoot one for

* See C.A.D.S. #2.

35

me. But the important thing is to avoid enemy contact. Get to the airdrome and fix that plane up to specs—you hear?"

"Can do!"

Then Martel and the eight technicians who would accompany him on the 262-mile Tri-bike journey to Arizona Airdrome roared into the cold December desert air.

The Arizona base, a camouflaged airstrip and hangar out in the mountains north of Flagstaff, was as secure a place as White Sands. But getting there— Sturgis worried about Martel.

Sturgis went back down the ramp as the steel doors slowly closed off daylight. He took the elevator to Assembly Area A, where he had ordered the inner circle—his C.A.D.S. officers—to convene. He would, of course, take these combat-hardened men with him on the mission. But not Sheila DeCamp. Doctors were too valuable. As for the other personnel for Project Talltree, he wanted the five officers' advice. There could be no slackers, no suicide-prone troopers in the group who would go to the Kremlin. The twenty men were already gathered, standing around conversing. They turned as he entered.

"Ten *hup!*" said Billy Dixon. They all fell into column and saluted.

"At ease," Sturgis said, giving a half salute in return to the men. He smiled warmly at the officers and their handpicked volunteers. It had been a long time since he had seen many of them—especially his inner circle of officers. They had been busy training new troopers or out on "sweep" assignments to the various new survival settlements.

Sturgis went down the line shaking each man's hand. First was Billy Dixon. His youthful looks and easy smile belied all his combat experience. The Southerner needed a shave. Sturgis, not one for military regulations, said nothing but a warm hello.

Then came Tranh, his oldest friend. Tranh and Sturgis went back a long way, and he didn't know what he'd do without his second in command—especially on such a mission as was now contemplated. The Vietnam-born Tranh had been up north near the Canadian border trying to whip into shape a survival colony. He had lost a few pounds and had a healing scar on his chin.

"Rough up there?" the colonel asked.

Tranh nodded. "A bit . . ."

Rossiter was looking fit and crisp in a heavily starched tan uniform, as he liked to be, and had a fresh haircut.

"Hi, Rossiter, glad to have you on board—where you been?"

"Just got back today from Frontier Five, Skip. That's down by Mexico—"

"How is it down there?"

"Great! Got the hydroponic tanks all set up to raise vegetables. And they now have six thousand sheep. My team collected and organized a hundred and fifty more farmers. The colony there is very spread out—but if there's a traitor among them . . ."

"Yeah—I know—it could all go the way of New City. That's why this mission is so important, Mickey."

He moved on down the line of nuke heroes to

Fenton MacLeish; the big Brit had grown a spiffy longish moustache on his beefy upper lip. He was as ruddy-faced as ever, and as stocky.

"Getting a bit round in the gut, Fenton?"

"Shot-put weight—all *hard muscle,*" he snapped, looking offended.

Fireheels, standing stiff and alert in his rawhide outfit, shook hands and said nothing.

A newly elevated from private Polish American trooper—Sergeant Wosyck—stood last in line. He saluted crisply.

"Glad to have you with us, Wosyck," the colonel said, feeling the tall thin man's strong grip. "Aside from ranking top of your class in C.A.D.S. suit operation, you speak fluent Russian—correct?"

"Yes sir!" His close-set brown eyes flashed with pride.

"What have you been doing since you made sergeant?"

"Sir, I haven't seen a ray of real sunshine for a month. Van Patten had me testing out some modifications on the Variable Shell-Fire system. I can report that the jamming problems are over. Now we can use almost any ammo we confiscate, and it'll feed right into the firing tubes."

"Great to hear that, Wosyck." Sturgis slapped him on the back. The man seemed a good choice. He'd be a big help.

After the colonel greeted the other volunteers, he said, "Now we get down to business—everyone sit down."

They all took their seats along the conference table. "Tranh, you were in charge of the L.W.A. task force. Have you licked the component shortage?"

"No. Skip. There aren't any 512 boards, or any B chips left in the whole Goddamned U.S.! But we have five of the old laser wave amplifier rifles—the ones that aren't reliable. Your decision to bring 'em or not."

Sturgis thought for a second. The unreliable weapons added weight. They would be too heavy enough with the other supplies. He remembered Sergeant Jamison raising his L.W.A. in battle to fire, and instead it blew up in his face sending him to bloody hell.

"We'll leave 'em behind," the colonel said. "How about you, Fenton? You check up on the new Tris?"

"Jolly right. And the news is a mix of bad and good, Skip. They will take low temperatures—but they will eat fuel, assuming we use oil or gasoline."

"Estimated range?"

"Fully fueled with number six oil—I'd say about a hundred and eighty miles—in subfreezing temperatures."

"That's not much—and fuel's a big problem—especially in our first days in Siberia. We might not find a place to steal fuel for hundreds of miles."

Rossiter spoke up. "It's worse than that. The tires on the Tris are heavier now. We had to make substitutions to have them withstand the cold. If there's a break in the ice—well, you asked me to look into their float capability. They'll sink."

"Damn," Sturgis muttered. "We're being confronted by low-tech problems at every turn. Pretty soon we'll be using clubs and spears!" He decided then and there: "The suits will get us to someplace we

39

can steal transport. Rossiter, we'll leave the Tris behind! Martel asked me to give him less weight for the plane trip. Feed the weight numbers on the Tris to Martel via radio, right after this meeting. He'll be mighty glad to know we're traveling lighter—gives him a safety margin on the Hercules range."

The colonel caught Billy and the others glancing occasionally at the door, so he said, "You're probably wondering why Dr. DeCamp isn't here. Well—she's not coming. Oh, I know she's a wonderful doctor and everything—and we all like her. But she's needed here. And let's face it: She doesn't check out well in the new suits. Their servo-mechanisms need more raw muscle power to operate them when the batteries are low. She'll have to stay behind. So, anyone have a line on a good substitute for medic?"

Wosyck spoke up. "Sir, there is Demmings, down in Level seven. The medic doing the study on the red-death disease. They'd hate to lose him, but he's a tough fighter. Demmings was a boxer once, has lots of muscle. And he's young—twenty-eight years old."

Sturgis said, "He'll do. We'll yank him, priority *one!* Now that we've decided on DeCamp's substitute—"

The door burst open, and a heavy breathing female cyclone was in its portal. "Dean! I don't know why you didn't invite me to this meeting. I have to check with you about the medical supplies! I should be here to know what to bring—"

"You're not coming," he snapped. "Sorry."

Sheila paled, took a step back then she said, "I HAVE to come!"

"It's a . . . technical problem . . . to bring you," Sturgis snapped, "nothing personal. We're bringing Demmings as our doctor."

"Demmings! Why he's the center of our red-death studies. You can't—" Her big blues flared wide in anger.

"I can! We're yanking him for the mission. Sorry, it's too important a mission to—"

"Whatever the hell the importance of the mission—I'm going to the president himself. I will tell him you can't leave me behind!"

She stormed out and slammed the door behind her.

Next Fireheels reported on the status of the Rhino all-terrain combat vehicle. "We can't take her, Skip. She has the same tire problems as the Tris. She used up all her regular rubber on the last mission. The weight of the new tires on the ice is prohibitive."

Sturgis nodded. "I counted on that being the case. I hadn't planned on bringing the Rhino anyway."

Fenton started to object.

"She's a dead giveaway. The lighter we travel, the better our chances. Sorry Fenton."

Sturgis looked down to the end of the table. "Billy! How about the snowshoes and the sleds?"

"We have the best of them ready." Dixon smiled. "But there's the little job of getting used to snowshoes. I tried the shoes out like you ordered, fully suited up. I went out on Powderdune, and I, er . . . fell a lot." He turned beet red.

The others laughed long and hard, but Sturgis didn't. He looked grim. "Gentlemen, we all have to learn to use the snowshoes. There's mostly snow and

41

ice all the way to Moscow, and I'm sure it isn't so hard once you get the hang of it. The suit's stabilizing system will help once it's adjusted. You don't have to be masters at it."

There were a few questions and answers and then Sturgis said, "While the drop-plane is being modified, our primary task is to learn how to trek with snowshoes on in the C.A.D.S. suit. The weight will be better distributed—to avoid falling through ice."

There was a collective groan.

"Resign yourselves to it. Well—what's next? Fireheels. Any suggestions about the route to Moscow from the drop site? Did you go over the maps and intel, like I asked?"

"Yes. It's a workable plan," the Indian said. "*If* we take the route along the Kamchatka Peninsula, in the time frame of . . ."

The meeting went on for five hours. All the men were exhausted when Sturgis summed up. "Men, I don't want gung-ho types on this mission. Billy is enough of those! I want follow-order types. Get your equipment fully checked out. And expect to come back. We wouldn't be going if there wasn't a chance—a good chance—of getting in and out. I want each man to believe firmly he will return. We can pull it off. There is the element of surprise on our side. It served us well in the past."

"You're right," Billy exclaimed enthusiastically. "The bastards would never think we're crazy enough to attempt something like this!"

Sturgis nodded, though he wished Dixon hadn't put it quite that way.

CHAPTER 5

It was time for Sturgis to say good-bye to Morgana. The report had come from Arizona that the plane was ready. As he walked down the long corridor toward her quarters he thought about the bizarre set of circumstances that had thrown the two together. Morgana was once the abused mistress of Pinky Ellis, the arch traitor.* Morgana had managed to escape the brutal fatman and make her way to White Sands. Now she was, in a way, White Sands's willing hostage; the oddest role of any woman since Helen of Troy. Pinky knew where White Sands base was, and normally he would have sold that info to the Russians. But he wouldn't, not as long as he knew Morgana Pinter was there. For Pinky wanted her desperately. Right now, Pinky and his mad army of mercenary killers were, Sturgis knew, somewhere out there in the desert, planning, scheming, to get in and take Morgana—alive.

* See C.A.D.S. #5.

Sturgis had slowly, inexorably, become her lover—a soft gentle lover, not an egomaniac degrader like Pinky. Morgana still bore many scars from the traitor's maltreatment—psychic as well as physical scars. The colonel hoped they would all fade.

Sturgis found her door, number 154, and knocked. The sound of running feet, the door swept open, and he was staring into her powder-gray eyes. Her expression of happy anticipation immediately changed. Morgana knew why he had come.

"It's that time?" she asked. He nodded. "Yes. Time to go."

"Where are you going? When will you be back?" Morgana let him in and closed the door.

"We agreed that we don't discuss my missions," he said softly.

"You're right. Should Pinky ever manage to recapture me, it would be better that I didn't know much."

"Not a chance he'll ever do that!" He crushed her to him. "We have the best security in the country here."

They kissed. When he pulled away, she asked wistfully, "Do you really think my presence is saving this base?"

"Yes darling." He crushed her in his arms again. "Stay here, wait for me. I'll be back, I promise."

"Is that woman doctor going with you?" There was sadness in her eyes.

"No, she's not," he reassured. "You don't have to worry about Sheila. She was a passing thing. We needed each other, out . . . there. You know how it is to need someone."

"Yes. And you should have anyone you want." She kissed him. "Just remember to come back to *me*."

"Always, dear. Always."

Morgana went to a dresser drawer, opened it, and extracted something. "Here," she said, "my scarf. Put it on under your C.A.D.S. suit." She handed him the gossamer maroon and gold scarf. He took it. It smelled of lilac, her perfume.

"Like the knights of old I'll wear my woman's colors." He kissed her and put it in his pocket.

Six hours later, Sturgis and his twenty-one troopers were in the giant six-engine Hercules C-131SP, taxiing down the hard-packed sand of the Arizona desert, into the strong western wind.

The plane looked a bit like a gooney bird, Sturgis had thought when he first saw her. Fat, slow, and heavy. Now, he wondered if she would fly. She was taking so long to get off the ground that he inwardly winced as he watched from the cabin window. But suddenly the ground noise ceased and the sixteen big tires left the earth. Gradually, the desert dotted with saguaro cacti fell away. The plane groaned higher and higher and then wheeled about, heading for the north and the polar regions. Sturgis leaned back and started to close his eyes.

"Surprise!" Out of a storage closet came Sheila DeCamp.

"Sheila! How the hell—what the hell? You're not supposed to be here!" Sturgis was shocked.

"Listen, Dean, and listen well," the feisty woman demanded, "I'm on this mission and that's that!" She glowered. As Sturgis renewed his objections, she snapped open a letter. "Here, read this. Orders from the president himself, saying that I am the medical person for this mission."

The colonel read the letter. It was exactly what Sheila had said. He looked up at her with trepidation in his gaze.

"Relax, I'm the best M.D. and psychiatric specialist on base."

"Well," Sturgis said, resigned to a fait accompli, "I can't say I'm not glad to have the best. What happened to Dr. Demmings, the M.D. that you bumped?"

Sheila tossed her wavy chestnut tresses back and smiled. "Why, he got a case of measles. I slipped and accidentally discharged a whiff of rubella-laden sample in his direction."

"You didn't!"

"Oh, but I *did*. You need me on this mission. I'm good luck; you said so yourself, many times."

His brown eyes met her deep blues. "Sheila, I wanted you to be—"

"Safe? Ha, that's a laugh in this world. I'll be safer where we're going, what with the Russians nuking half the west, and Pinky Ellis and his marauders on the loose." She took the seat next to him.

"But these C.A.D.S. suits aren't like the old ones.

46

They require more raw muscle power to operate. You don't have the muscle strength to operate them, Sheila."

She rolled up her black coveralls sleeve and made a bicep. "Stringy muscles, but muscles," DeCamp said proudly. "I've been working out Dean; I can hack it. Besides, I'm your personal physician." Sheila leaned her ample bosom into Dean and added in a husky whisper, "It gets cold sleeping alone in the arctic wastes."

"You've got it all figured out, huh?"

"Yes. Admit it, you're licked."

Sturgis nodded. Maybe they needed the woman's touch—as much as her medicines. He hoped the guys wouldn't be jealous if, on a cold night, he and Sheila kept warm. She caught his look and blushed. He smiled, "So I'm licked. But you're really in for it. There are a few things about how we get out of this plane that you might not be aware of!"

In three hours, the Hercules jet transport was cruising low over the frozen tundra of northern Canada. Together, Sturgis and Sheila DeCamp watched the arctic scenes slide by under the plane. The big shadow of the craft raced along, keeping it company.

"We're kinda low, aren't we, Dean?"

"Radar avoidance. The 'ground clutter' helps hide us off the Soviets' radar."

Then a herd of caribou, starled by their noise, began to run in patterns by the thousands across the

47

blue-white terrain.

"Oh, Dean, it's beautiful, isn't it?" Sheila remarked. They were staring out through a small half-frosted-over port. "I never thought there would be so many animals, or that ice could be in so many shapes."

"Pressure ridges," Sturgis explained. "It's all very explainable scientifically. But yes: It is beautiful! Now get the hell suited up, Sheila," he said, pushing her warm body away with reluctance. "We drop in twenty minutes."

"Skip," Billy called out walking down the wide cabin of the jet and coming over to the couple. "We have to turn back—they've forgotten to pack the parachutes for our drop."

"We're not using parachutes," the colonel said.

"No chutes? How the hell do we get down, if we can't land on the ice. We aren't landing, are we?"

"No, Billy. And we aren't using parachutes either. I didn't tell any of the team before, because it would have just made you all nervous. We're using Option A."

"What! Oh no!"

"Oh yes," frowned Sheila. "I just got the word. Hope you have a rabbit's foot for the both of us, Billy."

"But Skip," protested the platinum-haired Southerner. "Option A means we jump out of the plane in our C.A.D.S. suits at low altitude, and use the backpack jets to slow our fall. It's been done from a prop plane, at low speed. But never from a jet, except in a simulator!"

"Billy, there's a first time for everything. The

simulator proved it could be done. We all have jet backpacks. We can cut some of the forward momentum. This plane can get down to about two hundred miles per hour, about three hundred feet off the ice—well within training parameters."

"We have no choice," Sheila said grimly.

CHAPTER 6

They all had their C.A.D.S. suits on and were lined up. Sturgis went over the drop procedure one last time. Then the jump door slid open, letting the icy northern air into the plane. Billy, as usual, demanded that he go first. He stood in the open door, his gleaming black metal combat suit leaning into the howling arctic wind. They were all watching the frozen scenery whiz by three hundred feet below with apprehension. "Just keep those knees bent, Billy," Sturgis instructed. "And watch your jet-pack's fuel consumption."

"Yeah, Skip," the Southerner said on ampli-mode. "I'll do that."

"We dropped a flare last pass," Sturgis said. "That's the target. When you hit, bend your knees! I know you all don't like this very much. Neither do I. But it's this way down, or no way at all. Anyone can stay onboard if they want, and return to Arizona with the plane," Sturgis offered. "Just drop out of line."

No one moved out of the line. Sturgis smiled. "Then you're all birdmen! Good luck! Billy, get ready . . . go!"

The Southerner shouted, "I can't believe I'm doing this," as he jumped.

Sturgis watched Billy sail out the doorway, do a half-flip, stabilize, and ignite his backpack jet. As it began to slow the Southerner's descent, he dropped behind the plane. Then Sturgis himself jumped, Morgana's scarf clenched in his teeth.

"God!" he exclaimed as he whipped his legs into the right direction to fire the jet-pack. The icy ground was coming up too quickly, and his jets, on maximum, had a tough time decelerating him from 300mph toward the 10mph he needed to land. Plus he had trouble stabilizing, keeping his helmet pointed directly into the wake of the plane. But he managed and felt a certain joy.

"Easy . . . easy." He came along Billy and they were, for an instant, like two huge flying beetles. Then they made perfect feet-down landings, within yards of the flare. Billy didn't put his jets off quick enough, though, and tumbled end over end in the snow, hollering a blue streak of curses.

Sturgis went to Billy and helped him up. "Okay, man?" Sturgis asked. He wiped the caked snow off Billy's visor.

"Sure. Piece of cake!" They watched as the jet transport swung around and made another pass at the flare-lit jump site. Fenton, DeCamp, and Wosyck would jump on this pass. Sturgis listened to the shrill scream of Dr. DeCamp—nothing was wrong; she was just complaining. Sheila expertly completed the tricky landing maneuver, coming down on her feet, almost on top of Sturgis, fanning his suit with smoke as she cut off her jets a bit late. Hostility?

Wosyck hit snow twenty yards away from the flare, but Fenton landed just three feet from it, shouting in exaltation, "I'm closest!"

He was proven wrong by Tranh, when the Vietnamese-American dove from the plane with two other troopers on its third pass. Tranh's left foot nearly put the flare out! Wallace landed a few feet further from the target. Rossiter, the third man in that jump, to his chagrin, landed in a snow dune a hundred yards to the south. Cursing and swearing, the mechanic made his way toward the group of landed troopers. They all moved to the assembly area fifty yards south of the sputtering flare.

The next pass of the big transport jet proved less fortuitous. Dekes and Schwartz made it down okay, but Mendelson couldn't seem to get himself stabilized, and burned up too much fuel slowing down. He flamed out twenty feet up, landed so hard a shatter mark appeared on the ice. Sturgis thought for a second that the ice would give way, and that the man would drown. But Mendelson got up and staggered toward them waving, gasping, "Didn't think the helmet would hold!"

Sturgis was worried now—they had counted on the ice being six feet thick. After all, it was sixty below zero. But in some places, obviously, it wasn't thick at all. Should he call off the drop? No—too late, he decided. Just cross fingers.

A strong wind was now whipping at the gathered

C.A.D.S. soldiers, and Sturgis had to wipe the driven snow off his face plate to see the plane wheel around for another pass.

Again and again men fell in twos and threes, all landing safely—until the final two passes.

As the plane zoomed overhead at three hundred feet, the colonel watched Maswell, Dereksen, and Farrand come out of the plane's open door. As with the others, he could tell their identities only by accessing the I.D. mode on the suit computer. They wobbled down on their jets in the arctic half-light. They stabilized and slowed—except for Farrand. Sturgis immediately saw why. Only one of the two nozzles on Farrand's jet-pack had ignited.

"Equipment failure," the young man shouted, as he went spinning off like a pinwheel over an ice ridge.

Farrand was good. Sturgis watched him with Tele-I.R. mode as he tried to correct his direction. He was using his body well, swimming on the wind. Farrand had managed to reverse his direction despite his difficulties, and was headed back their way, a hundred and fifty feet off the ground, when his one active jet cut out. He hurtled downward at an alarming rate.

"Come on Billy," Sturgis shouted, "let's go get him." Their landings had been good, so they hadn't used up all their jet-pack's fuel. Sturgis and Billy hit the jets, hurling off in the direction of Farrand's fall.

Billy was somewhat ahead of Sturgis and managed to meet the falling dead weight of the distressed trooper ten feet up in midair. Billy shoulder-butted the man, like a circus clown would throw himself against a falling aerialist. The two metal figures clanged together mightily. Sparks actually flew. Sturgis landed, watched with heart pounding as Billy and Farrand tumbled to the snow. But the Southerner's bravery had saved the day. Aside from sore muscles, neither was hurt, it turned out.

"Good work," Sturgis complimented, helping Billy up.

"Yeah," Farrand said, standing up and straightening a bent helmet antenna with his metal gloves. "Thanks *mucho,* Billy."

They heard the drone of the big four-engine job again. It was coming around for the last drop. The colonel checked his chronometer. "Ten minutes late! Who hasn't dropped yet? What's the problem up there?"

The crackling reply from the pilot was, "Problem in Greenwald's jet-pack. Fireheels fixed it. They're both coming in on this pass with Mackintyre."

"Roger," Sturgis acknowledged, "make it good."

They watched the plane come around against a north wind. Then they saw three figures begin their fall. To their horror they watched as Fireheels and one of the recruits bumped into one another in midair. The I.D. mode showed it was Greenwald who hit Fireheels. Greenwald had jumped too soon after the Indian trooper. Now Fireheels went spinning out of control, his jet-pack sputtering, carrying him out over blue water. Out of range.

"Shit!" Billy exclaimed as they watched Fireheels splash down into the water and sink rapidly. Everyone knew that the Indian was a goner. The new

55

suits didn't have underwater capacity, nor would the jet-pack fire under water. Sturgis was stunned.

Billy sobbed out, "God! That means he's dead. Or will be, when his oxygen runs out."

Sturgis's mind balked, yet what was there to do except to carry on? The fate of the world hung in the balance. Fireheels's death must not be in vain! "Come on. Let's get to the others. They might need help," he said with a tremble in his voice. "Nothing we can do about Fireheels." He cleared his throat, ordered in his gruffest voice. "Use 'rapid-walk,' don't use the jet-packs. Come on. Greenwald might be hurt."

The others glumly fell in beside Sturgis. "I.D. mode," Sturgis commanded, "Computer, give status of two descended C.A.D.S. men. Compute their landing zone."

John Mackintyre, Manny Greenwald," the readout came back. *Two landed in proximity, six hundred yards southwest. Impact speed twenty KM/HR. Health status . . . Acceptable.*

"That's impossible," Sturgis huffed, pushing his legs against the servo-mechanism assist-drives in the C.A.D.S. outfit's legs. "Greenwald must be hurt!" Sturgis wanted someone he could help.

They climbed over a snow ridge and came to a jumble of twisted spirelike ice formations. It was a pretty place, but disturbingly alien at the same time. The sickening feeling of loss of his dear friend Fireheels threatened to overwhelm Sturgis. He just wanted to sit in the snow and weep. But there was work to be done. The mission must go on.

"Radar mode, search for Mackintyre, Greenwald," Sturgis ordered his computer.

Two troopers fifteen yards west of current position, the computer readout came back.

They bounded toward the location indicated and found nothing. "Why can't we see or hear them?" Billy asked. "What's going on?"

"Computer must be on the fritz, giving the wrong drop location," Sturgis decided. But when accessed, the computer said they were here.

The solution to the problem was suddenly obvious. Sturgis shouted, "They must have fallen so hard—they're buried!" He yelled, "Radar mode—probe snow below for trooper location."

The surface-piercing readout indicated that the two fallen troopers were *ten feet straight down.*

"Quick, start digging," the colonel ordered. "We've got to save them!"

As he helped the others dig, using power-assist metal hands like mad snow shovels, Sturgis felt a wave of nausea. Fireheels—dead! It couldn't be. And, if it were true, if Fireheels had "bought it," it was his fault. Sturgis was the one who had this hair-brained polar trek idea in the first place. He ceased digging.

After a moment of stunned paralysis, he unfroze. "Keep scanning for Fireheels, everyone—and let's dig these guys out!"

The two buried troopers were pulled out of their ice graves in short order. They appeared to be okay, once they brushed themselves off and got their antennas working. Then the four man party headed back toward the assembly area. Never were men so glum.

*　　　*　　　*

As soon as they had joined the others, Sturgis started to shout orders. "DeCamp! Check these two guys out—and anyone else who feels he has a medical situation." He looked up.

One glance at the turgid, darkening sky showed that they were about to undergo a bad snowstorm. Sturgis said, "You all have been monitoring developments. You know what happened. Fireheels is presumed dead. He broke through thin ice and sank. We can only assume the worst, but keep scanning on all modes. If nothing turns up . . ." He sighed deeply. "There will be a brief memorial service—later. As soon as the lean-to and the microwave heater is set up. Get to work. Continue the mission!"

CHAPTER 7

Thanks to the sickening blow of Greenwald's C.A.D.S.-armored body impacting against him, Joe Fireheels had felt himself spinning out of control, his jet-pack busted. No matter what he did, Fireheels had realized he was going to come down hard. Too hard.

As his jet-pack flamed out, Fireheels saw the dots of black on the surface of the ice below whiz by. Those were his friends! Then he passed over an ice ridge, his speed still near 300mph.

Could he bring himself under control? No chance. The ice ground was rushing up sideways. He bent his head over so that his visor wouldn't take the first-contact impact. Then he saw blue. Water! A stunning blow, then blackness.

Floating . . . What? Darkness . . . Am I dead? No. No!

Fireheels came slowly to his senses. No—it wasn't

death's darkness. It was water. "God . . . I'm under water!" he exclaimed. The emergency readout's purple print was on *depth 21 meters, . . . descending, 1 meter per second.*

Fireheels shouted, "Release SMG, eject jet-pack."

There was a rush of bubbles around him. Still sinking. But more slowly. Water dribbled into the suit through a dozen joints. He waited until his level indicator showed he was floating head up, then pointed his right weapons arm down and said, "Fire all shells, quarter-second intervals. Now."

Sixteen C.A.D.S.-type 30mm shells rocketed out into the water, before the *system abort* readout started blinking. He had gotten some propulsion upward, but now the firing mode was kaput!

Depth 30 meters, said the computer's purple readout, *Twenty-nine meters, 28 meters, 28.5 meters.*

Not enough; his rise was slowing.

Drops of water were now creeping along his faceplate on the inside. Fireheels felt wetness on his legs, too. The icy water. Soon he would be weighted down with it. He had to do something else now, while some suit systems still worked. But what? Fireheels tried to swim—a powerful backstroke— while the suit servos could still function.

Good. *Depth 26 meters, 25 . . ."* He was making slow progress.

Electrical shorts halted his efforts. Darkness; then the constant familiar hum of the suit died. Silence. A watery grave, the Indian fighter thought. "This is it." He smiled to himself as his life passed before his eyes. Mother; Father; joining the service . . . More water coming in now. He knew he was sinking, thought there was no readout on his suit's visor.

No hope.

Fireheels called to the Great Spirit. "It is I, Fireheels, your son, oh Great Spirit, who ask you to let me live. I must live to serve the earth—the precious mother of all. I will fight the enemies of the wholeness, I pledge, Wankapatanka."

Water was up to his waist now in his suit, and getting higher rapidly. This was—

No!

A bump against his feet. What the hell? In the total darkness, he bent, groping, in the inky water— and grabbed something slippery and massive.

Hold on! Hold on! There were no more servos to assist him, just his steely grip. Hold on hard as you can.

It was a smooth, rubbery thing that he held, and it was rising. Rolling back and forth, but rising. Yes, he was sure it was going up!

Fireheels was getting close enough to the surface now to see light and broken slabs of ice. Plus he could see what he was holding. He nearly let go—but didn't—when he saw that he was hanging on for dear life to the fin of a huge black and white sea beast!

The creature was rushing up toward the air. There was water at his neck; a spray from a crack in the visor. But no matter! Suddenly they were out, and then up in the air! Fireheels saw now that the thing he clung to was a sixty-foot-long killer whale. It rose forty or fifty feet and slowly, in midair, it twisted to shake him off—and he let it.

Fireheels sailed out in an arc and over solid ice.

Then he slammed into that ice. His visor cracked, and water spilled out. He sucked in a breath of intensely cold arctic air. He was alive!

Fireheels turned to see the creature dive into the depths once more. Then he slid like a wounded seal across the ice to avoid the huge wave. Utterly exhausted, he lay there a long time. His prayer to the Great Spirit had been answered, he realized. By one of its great creatures. Wankapatanka, Great Spirit, is everywhere.

He wanted to just lie there and breathe. But he knew he couldn't. The water in his suit was already freezing. Fireheels forced himself up on his left knee, then his right. Fighting exhaustion, and the cold, he stood up.

Fireheels started walking. So cold. So cold. So hard to move his legs. The water in his suit had quickly become chunks of ice. He was literally packed in ice! And yet, against the wind, in ice coveralls, he staggered on. Without the suit, he reasoned, he'd be even colder. He tried to restart the systems to no avail. He tried the radio every thirty seconds. Nothing. The antennae were a bent mess; even if he could get power up, it wouldn't work.

Would he die anyway? Die after this miracle of the Great Spirit? Would the Great Spirit rescue him, only to let him die on the ice?

CHAPTER 8

The C.A.D.S. troopers were huddled in a circle in the dark, like some prehistoric shadows against the aurora's moving electric sky curtain. They were gathered around the dull orange glow of the microwave heat cell. The three-foot high, cylindrical machine was far from being a real campfire, but it gave to the somber men gathered about it sort of the same feeling, because it glowed. Actually, the device's heat was transmitted to the suits, saving their precious power packs. Sturgis, despite the warming effect, felt numb, like some sort of unfeeling zombie of the Arctic. Inside the silence of his metal suit he wept—wept for his friend Fireheels. And surely, he thought, this was a bad omen for the whole mission. But they would go on, he resolved. Fireheels would want them to go on.

They huddled under the flickering aurora's colors, warming themselves for a long time, before the colonel spoke. He said. "Perhaps . . . I could now say a few words about our lost friend."

There was a murmer of acquiescence.

"First of all, Joe Fireheels was the best of fighters. Also . . . he was intelligent and brave. He was . . ." The colonel's voice broke. "Goddammit! Why did he have to die like this? We don't even have his body!"

Suddenly Sturgis's search-scan started beeping. *Unidentified intruder located. Twenty-one degrees south by southwest, distance two miles.*

"Two miles! Who the hell . . ." the colonel exclaimed.

A crackling static-filled transmission started coming on the radio, too garbled to understand.

"Computer, clarify transmission being received."

There was a buzz and a playback, still too garbled to understand. "Red alert," Sturgis said. "Cut off the heater, Tranh. Everyone check weapons systems." He could see a blue triangle on the screen now—a hostile! The suit-computer readout indicated, *One armor-suited soldier.*

Sturgis, the consummate commander, dished out a menu of orders: "Billy, take three men, go up on that ice ridge to the right. Tranh, Fenton, come with me—up on the left hill. We'll blast this guy from both sides. He must be a Soviet gray suit scout!"

Shortly, Sturgis was atop the frozen hillock, scanning visually for the lone intruder. He was facing right in the direction of the low sun and there was an ice fog. Nevertheless, the slow-moving figure could be dimly discerned.

"Get ready to fire long range E-balls, men," Sturgis ordered. On my command—*Wait!*"

"What's the problem, Skip!" came Billy's southern drawl. "I've got the gray suit lined up."

"It's not a gray suit! It's—one of ours! All beat up, dented, but . . ."

"God!" Tranh yelled. "The blue I.D. turned to red on my screen. It must be . . ."

"I'm alive," Fireheels said, his words nearly lost in transmission chop. "Damaged my antennae. Don't know if you can hear me! Have you located. Making my way there."

"*Fireheels,*" the colonel shouted. "How did you get out of the water?"

Fireheels's reply was studded with static. "*Bzzz— easy Skip . . . bzzz bzzz . . . you help me?*"

"Computer, tele-mode—zero in on Fireheels," Sturgis ordered. He began a loping run down the hill toward the distant figure. His visor slowly swung and steadied on an ethereal wraithlike blacksuit floating like a mirage on the ice fog, as if it were above the frozen blue waste. Tranh, too, was heading for Fireheels. They reached Fireheels just as he was collapsing, and caught him under each metal arm. Pulling the metal-clad warrior erect, they beheld his ice-coated features, which bore a little half-smile. Then, his eyes rolled up.

"He's passed out, Tranh," Sturgis said. "Help me carry him back to the base. Sheila—you ready for hypothermia treatment?"

"Roger, Skip," came her clear female voice in his com-speaker.

CHAPTER 9

DeCamp was out of her metal suit and in her work coveralls. She had the survival tent ready with blankets and the portable microwave heater by the time Sturgis and Tranh had Fireheels back. She shooed the men away after they deposited Fireheels—still encased in his icy C.A.D.S. suit—inside the tent. Working quickly, she zipped up the tent and raised the light in the Coleman lamp. Fireheels was unconscious but she spoke to him anyway. "I'm raising the temperature in your suit slowly, by the rule book, using the microwave heater. Then I'll open you up . . ." She first made sure he was still breathing by holding a mirror to his purple lips. He was. Then, choking down a sob of relief, she started picking pieces of magna-glass from his shattered visor plate out of his face. "Nothing in your eyes," she muttered. "You're lucky."

Sheila saw the ice was melting on his neck—slowly. Five minutes later, she took the helmet off. The temperature in the tent was forty degrees and she shivered, but she wanted to take the proper time. "No sense losing you now, Fireheels." Amazingly, his metal-gloved hand moved and grabbed her wrist. "I'm not dead," he mumbled through purplish lips.

"No," she smiled warmly. "Of course not."

Fireheels, when he ate breakfast in the open with the others the next morning, refused to explain how he had managed to survive. He just shrugged and said, "Luck." That was all they could get from him. Another bizarre episode in their travels with Fireheels.

Eventually, they gave up their questioning, and the subject changed to what they would do next.

"We lost a lot of our food supplies," Martinson reported. "The plane dropped the tow-sled in the water."

Fireheels said, "There are tracks of animals in the snow, but I assume that hunting is out. We don't want to make noise, correct, Skip?"

"Correct. But hopefully, we're not that far from Mother Russia, where we'll steal what we need. I expect we can make the hundred miles in three days. I suppose we could fish on the way, but we don't have any lines—or traps."

Billy cut in. "Hey, maybe you could come up with something for us, Fireheels. You mentioned once that you did a lot of ice fishing before the war."

"I can do better than that," the Indian said. "I packed some harpoons and a few bows and arrows in with the ammo-supply cartons."

"That was good thinking," said Sturgis, "but I'd

68

rather move fast and get to the mainland. We can hunt or fish if we see anything. But no time out to track animals, my friend, as much as I'd like to."

"Agreed. As we get closer to land," Fireheels suggested, "there should be more animals, and one of us will hit his mark."

"Now just a bloody minute there, Fireheels," Fenton interjected. "How many harpoons and bows do you have?"

"Three of each. I was hoping for volunteers to learn bow and harpoon. If anyone wants on-the-hunt-training—"

A dozen voices rose to volunteer.

The first day's trek was in good weather; the ice was firm, and they made over thirty-five miles.

They bedded down for the night, burrowing into their quickly made ice cave. It was amazing how warm an ice home could be. Soon the temperature actually went above the freezing mark. Fenton filled his canteen and made them all warming tea from the runoff trickle of the wall. They left the heater on low.

The colonel was amazed when he opened his eyes to a dim morning light. He didn't remember shucking his suit, rolling out the bedroll, going to sleep at all—he had been exhausted.

There was no breakfast except coffee. The men gathered around Sturgis for instructions. "Order of the day. Some of us go ahead and procure chow," Sturgis intoned.

"Password, 'cheeseburgers,'" Fenton joked.

"Fireheels," Sturgis asked, "select two men for harpoon and bow training."

Fireheels said, "Okay. I know you all want to try. Anybody ever hunt with harpoon? Anyone good with a bow?"

Nobody responded.

"Well, Billy, and, er . . . you, Rossiter, are my choice for instant hunters," said Fireheels.

Billy nodded. "Sounds like fun."

Rossiter threw his hands up in the air. "I'd rather use the SMG. What do we hunt?"

"Caribou tracks out there," Fireheels said. "Very tasty. But hard to hit."

"Better than this pemmican, anyway, I'll bet," Billy added, throwing down his last "Fenton-mocha" into the snow. "Show me the bow and arrows!"

After the hunters moved out, the others packed up the gear and followed. They would take turns pulling the remaining sled of ammo supplies.

The suit computers soon gave barometer warnings.

"Damn," Sturgis said aloud. "The weather doesn't look good!" His foreboding came true, for as soon as the pale sun dipped below the horizon, and it was twilight again, the winds picked up. The sky became heavy and overcast. An ice fog would have made any movement forward impossible, but with their I.R. on maximum, they trudged on. "Barometer falling like a broker on Black Monday, Sturg," Fenton reported.

"Yeah." The colonel called back the three hunters and all together again—for safety—they went onward.

In the gathering gloom, the metal-clad warriors bent into the sudden blast of wind-driven snow. The only sound was the wind whistling through the C.A.D.S. suits' antennas. Sturgis had hoped they could keep their visors up and breathe the air—but the temperature soon was minus thirty degrees. It was not supposed to be this cold, according to data from Arctic expeditions. They were already using thirty percent more power than they had planned for, and Sturgis worried about that. Fireheels's visor plate had been replaced from their parts supplied, but his suit had only been patched.

"How's your suit, Joe," he asked on the com.

"Good enough, Skip," the Indian replied. His mike was clear at least, even if some other of his systems still were down.

Sturgis, gritting his teeth, said, "Good, I hope this storm ends soon so we can let your team hunt us down some decent food."

"Roger."

It was almost totally dark; they used their helmet lights. Three hours of daylight was hardly his idea of a full day! They trekked on, guided by their geo-compasses and scanner. Two hours into the storm there was something disturbing. That, the colonel felt more than detected.

"Does something—the ground—feel funny to you, Tranh?" Sturgis asked.

"Now that you mention it, it does."

"Computer, scan depth of ice."

Scanning . . . three point one meter.

"Damn, the ice is getting thinner and thinner!"

"Yeah Skip," Billy chimed in. "And the stuff is shaking, too!"

"Skip," Tranh called, "I'm getting a two point one Richter shake, coming from the southeast."

"What's that?"

"An earthquake!"

"It's an icequake, Billy," DeCamp explained. "Much worse than an earthquake—for us. It's caused when waves build up under the ice. I read about polar expeditions in school. Storms can generate waves under the ice—that's what we're feeling."

"Is it going to break up, Sturgis?" Billy worried aloud. "I can feel it in my legs. The ice is rolling!"

Sturgis, too, felt it clearly now; it was getting hard to move forward without lurching, so lurch he did. The C.A.D.S. troopers were worried, but their commander answered all their anxious statements with the same reply: "Just keep walking, men. Nothing we can do about it. Pray that it doesn't get so bad that the ice opens up under us."

Nobody uttered another word. They walked on in the darkness for hours, until the rolling and huge snapping noises in the distance subsided. Finally the shaking stopped. The instruments told Sturgis that they had barely made ten miles. "Computer," Sturgis ordered, "probe for depth of ice."

Seven meters.

"That's good," Sturgis said with relief. "This is our campsite," he said, surveying the tumble of twisted ice formations ahead. "It's getting light again and there's ice fog. We'll get lost in this white jumble— and there's another storm coming, according to the barometer! We'll build an ice shelter. Billy, Tranh, come help me. Use your flame modes on this wall of ice here." Sturgis gave the command to fire and the three men directed the powerful flames from their incendiary weapons, quickly boring a deep glistening cavern in the side of the cliff. They advanced into the opening, carving out a comfortable niche, while being careful to leave columns of ice every ten feet or so to support the mountain of snow overhead. When they had finished a thirty-foot room, they cut a small gully to let the water from the melted ice flow out, and began to move in. "It'll do nicely," said Fenton, impressed with his teammates' handiwork. "I'll make the last tea up. Did you ever hear the joke about . . ."

Some eight hours later, the C.A.D.S. team reemerged rested, if hungry. They packed up the supplies, and moved on in clear weather. Sturgis went ahead with Fireheels and found a pass through the ice-ridge hills. And Fireheels found something else. "Skip, we're right on a bunch of animal tracks," he said. "I think they're caribou."

"You want to go hunting now?"

"We have to, Skip. It's not really optional now. It's a necessity. We've consumed a lot of calories that have to be replenished if we're going to have the strength to go on."

"You're right. Let's full-power up your three hunters' suits so you can really move," Sturgis said. "We can transfuse our power to you, Billy, and Rossiter. Get your auxiliary hookups out and call your team together. Tell Fenton and Tranh to meet us, too, so they can help supe you guys up."

When the other C.A.D.S. members had caught up with Sturgis and Fireheels, the colonel gave his orders. "I'll full-power up Fireheels. Fenton, you take Rossiter; and Tranh takes Billy. Give them everything but ten percent of your reserves."

Billy objected. "We don't need full power to hunt. You guys won't have enough power to even keep warm."

"We'll manage with the microwave heater. If you guys can bring back some food worth eating, it'll be well worth it."

The couplings were made, and like blood donors, the C.A.D.S. men transfused power to their companions via the jumper cables attached to each man's power transfer receptacle on their arms. Ten minutes later, two of the hunters' suits were at ninety percent power. Rossiter's batteries didn't respond. Fireheels, to Mickey's annoyance, picked Sal Martinson as his replacement. Martinson's suit was charged.

"Now get the hell out there and bag something. Try to use Fireheels's equipment," Sturgis said. "But if it's necessary, use the SMG mode. Just bring us back something."

The team of three armored hunters took up their bows and arrows and moved out. The colonel and his companions watched them move out through the ice fog. They looked weird—and laughable. Space-age warriors in high-tech nuke combat gear wielding bows and arrows.

"Be back in a flash with lunch," Billy promised optimistically.

CHAPTER 10

Fireheels, Martinson, and Dixon were six miles ahead of the others, following the tracks of three arctic caribou. Fireheels said, "We might see them very soon. Everyone keep alert." They moved along, black metal intruders in an ice wonderland. About one hundred yards further on amidst delicate spires of ice crystal, there was an abrupt end to the tracks. And there was blood on the snow. Fresh, congealing blood. The whole area was torn up, as if a struggle had occurred.

"Something has gotten to them ahead of us," Billy said, looking around. "And that something had big teeth. It had to be—"

"Yeah," Martinson finished, "something big, like a polar bear."

Fireheels tried to report to Sturgis, but the com didn't work.

It was Fireheels who first noted that there was a heavy ten-foot wide drag trail on the ice, heading toward the ridge to the west. "Whatever ate the caribou was something without a set of legs," the Indian said matter-of-factly.

"What could it be? A snake?" Billy asked, dry-mouthed.

"Don't make me laugh. An ice snake?" Martinson said. "It's just a—"

"Well, we'll just have a look see," Fireheels decided. "We should find out." He had a bad feeling as they followed the wide, deep drag mark spotted with blood. His fears were well founded.

They turned a corner and, in the center of a hundred-yard-wide craterlike crystallized ice area below them, stood a gray-black blubbery shape; a massive-tusked walrus, perhaps twenty feet long. Billy accidentally dislodged some ice and the thing heard it fall and turned toward them, dropping the head of the caribou in its jaws on the bloody snow. It bellowed out a challenge.

It had dozens of extra flippers, as many as a caterpillar has legs. These enabled it to quickly build up speed in its mad kill-run toward the three humans. Its immense jaws opened and shut as it ran; it was practicing devouring what it soon would encounter.

"It's coming straight at us!" Billy yelled. "Forget the bows and arrows. Prepare SMG mode."

"What the hell is it!" Martinson gasped, lifting his weapons-arm.

"Some sort of a giant walrus," Billy guessed. "And he's after our meat!"

They watched it come at them. The animal was gathering speed, using its many traction flippers like snowmobile treads to propel itself forward.

"Better use E-balls," Fireheels ordered. "In sequence."

"But we're not supposed to make any noise! The Russians . . ." Martinson stuttered.

"Screw the noise!" Billy exclaimed. "Prepare to shoot!"

They lined up on the thing. It was fifty, forty, thirty yards away, and its slavering jaws seemed yards wide. The polar monster didn't seem to be losing any speed on the upslope either, making forty miles per hour according to the readouts in Fireheels's helmet.

The Indian squad leader saw his E-ball system lights flare and he shouted, "Okay, fire!"

Nothing happened! Their weapons system aborted.

"Electrical failure in the tubes!" Fireheels shouted. "Switch to . . ."

He never had to finish, for the others were already firing their SMGs on manual override. But the explosive 9mm bullets hitting the thing bounced off, like pebbles thrown against a locomotive!

The walrus thing was now just a few feet from them; they pumped round after round of shells at its thick, rubbery hide.

"Shoot its eyes!" Billy and Fireheels—whose SMG mode now functioned—concentrated their fire on the thing's yellow, saucerlike eyes. They burst like a set of water-filled globes. The thing roared and lurched violently, but continued blindly forward. It smelled out Martinson and hit him with a powerful smack from its head, sending the man crashing into a rocklike ice mound. In a second, the

77

creature plunged its ironlike tusks right through the C.A.D.S. warrior, by chance hitting the vulnerable junction where the helmet meets the body of the suit. The tusk drove through and a gusher of blood shot forward. The walrus was able to tear the luckless Martinson's head from his body, bellowing its rage.

Billy and Fireheels had the beast concentrated in a volley of crossfire, pummeling its head with heavy doses of lead. They walked slowly toward it, impervious to the horror of their comrade's fate, professionally tending to the destruction of the enemy by blasting its torn eye sockets.

Finally, after what seemed like an eternity, the thing's head was just a pulp of mushed flesh atop its body. The creature's attack was over. It slumped over dead, still clutching remnants of Martinson's flesh in its teeth.

The two surviving C.A.D.S. men backed away from the broken corpse of their friend and the pile of twitching, blubbery, bloody monster, as if disbelieving.

"Wh . . . what do we do?" Billy asked.

"Poor Martinson," Fireheels said. "I guess . . . we bury him."

The C.A.D.S. troopers some miles away from the hunters heard the shots. "Too much firing for just a few caribou," Tranh said. "What do we do?"

"We hold up here," the colonel said. He looked around them. There were tall spindles of strangely pink ice all around, and the ice under their feet was crazed with cracks like a thousand-year-old ceramic

78

plate. The computer said it was thick ice, but Sturgis swore he could see water right through the semi-transparent stuff.

"This place is weirder than I thought the ice cap would be," Tranh said in understatement. "I expected just some flat ice and lots of snowstorms."

Sheila came up to Sturgis and pressed her visor release. "I've shut off my radio. Can you do the same?" she asked. Sheila had a worried look in her blue eyes.

Sturgis shut off the com and opened his own faceplate. They walked a bit away from the others, then he spoke.

"What's up, Sheila?"

"Dean, I think those shots could mean trouble."

"Reds?"

She bit her lip. "Worse. Have you noticed how weird the landscape is around here? And the weather is off, too. Changes too rapidly."

"What are you hinting at?"

"Radiation. Though I haven't picked it up yet, I think—"

"Well—suppose some of the missiles that flew at the U.S. didn't make it. They crash here at the pole, and they don't go off, but leak. It's one explanation for the change in the ecosystem here. And it could . . ." She let it go unsaid, but the colonel picked up on the thought.

Grimly, he said, "Those shots could be our men confronting another change in the ecosystem. Some mutant animal . . ."

"It's happened before. Wherever there's radiation, there's changes in the gene structure of plants

79

and animals."

The colonel thought a moment. "That's not the worst danger, Sheila. If you're right about stray nuke warheads out there—they could go off. If the ice shifts and disturbs them. Thanks for the talk on the Q.T., Sheila; I'm going to speed us up, go all out to get us off this ice pack! And send men ahead now to check up on our hunters."

CHAPTER 11

Before Sturgis could order a search for them, Joe Fireheels and Dixon came back to the others on the run. They were greeted with cheers; everyone thought they were returning with meat for dinner. The cheering died down when they noticed one man was missing.

"Where's Martinson?" Sturgis asked, a sickening feeling tightening his gut.

Billy spilled out the entire tragedy on audi-mode. "A monster walrus—I think that's what it was— attacked us. It was nearly bulletproof. Martinson's dead! We tried to use our E-ball systems in sinc-mode to destroy it, but they malfunctioned. I don't know if it's the separate systems or the linkup function that aborted. We switched to SMG and finally killed it. But not until it was too late."

"Do you think there are more of them, Fireheels?" the colonel asked, turning to the Indian officer.

"If there are we'd better get the hell out of here, double quick," Fireheels replied.

"Why didn't you radio for help?" Tranh asked.

"This is the first time we've been able to hear you guys on our radios. There's terrific interference out there. It got even worse just before the walrus attack."

"There was all this jamming of our systems too," Billy added. "It knocked out all my scan-modes. I only got readings on my screens a few hundred yards from here. Skip, the thing that killed Martinson was big as a tank and its teeth, or tusks, cut right through his armor! Martinson fought to the end!"

"We covered up what was left of Martinson," Fireheels added somberly, "with chunks of ice."

"All right," Sturgis said in a comforting tone. "May his soul rest in peace. He was a soldier, and a brave man."

The C.A.D.S. force observed a moment of silence for their fallen comrade before moving on. Sturgis took a deviation from their planned path. After a while, Rossiter spoke up. "Skip—a walrus that size—do you think it was a radiation mutant?"

"Yes," Sturgis replied. "What they ran across was an atomic mutation for sure. I hadn't expected them—up here. We've run into similar mutations before. Remember the rad-roaches around the bombed western cities?* I want to keep a mile east of where that mutant beast was, even if we're running late."

"Shouldn't we pack the walrus meat before we move on?" Fireheels asked as they passed closest they would come to the scene of the encounter.

"Forget it," insisted Sheila DeCamp. "I just did a

* See C.A.D.S.—the first book.

geiger sweep west. That thing is in the area of a high rad source. It's practically off the scale! And Dean, our two hunters are hot, too!"

Upon hearing that, Sturgis immediately halted the column. He had the two men who had encountered the beast stand in front of him. Sturgis doused them with his LPF flame-mode for thirty seconds to decontaminate them. Their suits were scoured to three hundred degrees then DeCamp checked them with the geiger.

"They're clean," she said. "Good thing the suits are flameproof."

"Yeah," replied Sturgis. "Now let's make some time."

After two days of exhausting trekking, the troopers were done in. They had had no food worth speaking of for thirty-six hours. Their suits' heat functions, due to lack of power, were down to thirty-two degrees. The men with the greatest endurance, Fenton, Rossiter, Dixon, and Tranh, pulled the ammo and supplies sled slower and slower. Over sixty miles of ice to go!

Sturgis felt as low as he ever had in his entire life. He felt he had already botched the mission. The trek over the ice cap to avoid Soviet radar appeared to be a serious miscalculation. They hadn't even seen the enemy yet, and he had lost one man, and the others were dead on their feet. The equipment was breaking down in the intense cold, and their firing systems were so adversely affected that they were practically defenseless. And there were monsters out there, plus they had no food!

But still, the only thing to do was to go on. So he would do his best to keep them moving.

Finally, the geo-compass in Sturgis's suit indicated they were less than six miles from the Siberian coast. He halted the column and climbed an ice hillock. The colonel scanned the horizon with tele-mode and infrared. Again ice fog and mirage-like images made viewing difficult. "There!" he exclaimed. "Those bumps on the horizon are real! They're solid rock mountains, not Goddamn illusions! The readings confirm."

Fireheels ran up alongside him to have a look. Seconds later he confirmed, "Yeah, they are. But Skip, there's a mile of churning water between our ice flow and the coast. Did you see that, too?"

"That's what we have the collapsible coracles along for," Sturgis said. "They'll get us across."

"I don't trust them," Fireheels said. "I don't trust the water."

"I'm sorry, Joe. We'll have to cross the water."

Shortly, they were at the edge of the ice. The troopers rolled out the paper-thin ultra-steel sheets that were the supports for the coracles and clipped the thin metal fabric into the plastic expanding staves from the boat kit. The result was two unsteady-looking thirteen-foot-long by six-foot-wide canoe-type boats that sat on the ice, rocking in the wind.

"These two things look like boats," Fireheels said, "but they aren't. They'll break."

"Don't let the thinness and lightness of the material fool you, Fireheels," said Sturgis in a voice more confident than he felt. "This stuff is durable, no matter how thin and flimsy it looks. Get them into the water, men; it's the only way to get to solid land."

"Amen for solid land," DeCamp said with tiredness racking her voice, "even if it is the Soviet Union!"

There was only one way to get into the coracles without capsizing them. The C.A.D.S. soldiers—half in the first boat, the others in the one alongside it—got in while the boats were still on the ice. Then they used the aluminum oars to push the boats off the ice shelf, splashing brazenly into the Siberian waters. Sturgis prayed silently that he was right when he said there was no chance the things wouldn't just rip and sink like a rock.

When they hit the water and they didn't sink, he felt an overwhelming sense of relief. "Man those oars!"

Quickly paddling away from the ice, the metal-clad sailors strove to fight the southward current and get to the rocky shore ahead of them, half lost in mist. They were the oddest-looking Vikings, Sturgis thought. Their all-metal boats were shiny silver, like aluminum foil, and the black-metal C.A.D.S. men rowing each coracle with the aluminum oars whirred and clanked with each mechanical push. They rowed with all their considerable power-armed might, and soon the boats were making progress, but heading sideways, at the coastline.

The heavily laden coracles rocked and rolled in

the choppy gray seas, but didn't take on any water. Sturgis started to believe that they would make it after all. They were three-quarters of the way to the shore. R and D had done its job well!

"Less than a hundred and fifty yards to go!" he called, encouraging his men.

"We're gonna land on that rocky part of the shore," Billy said. "I could kiss Van Patten! These coracles are his brainchild!"

"If we don't roll over first," DeCamp worried. She sounded seasick, and a cross-check on her health readouts showed pulse irregular.

As they approached within fifty yards of the shore the coracles started to bounce and roll in breakers that were oceanlike in intensity. The first boat, Billy's "yacht" as he called it, sprung a leak. "Cancel the kiss," Billy exclaimed.

Sturgis called out to his rowers: "Men, steer toward Billy's coracle, He's taking on water. Come around on the port side," Sturgis yelled, "and lash our boat to his."

They rowed like *mothers* and quickly pulled alongside the badly listing boat, lashed cables onto her to make the vessel more stable.

Billy and two of the men were down at the six-inch tear in the boat's bottom, frantically working to place a fiberglass patch over it—there was an emergency repair kit on board each boat. Other men were bailing out the water with their mess-kit canteens. The patch was secured in a few minutes; all the while the two vessels proceeded, lashed together.

As they began their final approach to land, the waves again erupted violently, threatening to overturn the boats.

"Row! Row like galley slaves!" Sturgis snapped. "Or we check our suits into Davy Jones's locker!"

The battered coracles smashed ashore on the back of an immense breaker, and broke to pieces on the rocks. Sturgis thought, *This is the end.* But fate had it that the wave had deposited them so high on a bouldered beach that the following smaller breakers merely flooded knee-deep around the troopers scrambling for higher ground.

The men grabbed the loose equipment and fell exhausted on a gravel slope above the rocky beach, glad to be alive.

"I can't believe it! We all made it without even losing any ammunition," Billy said with relief. "And the equipment is dry!"

Fenton disagreed. "Not quite! My bagpipes are a wee bit wet!" He held his plaid bag and pipes up. They made a mournful sound as they dripped seawater and bowed over.

Sturgis said, "Don't worry, Fenton. We'll fix 'em for you."

They all laughed. Laughed as only the doomed, suddenly freed from imminent death, can laugh.

CHAPTER 12

Slowly, the exhausted C.A.D.S. troopers rose and formed up. The stronger ones helped the weak. They had to get moving or die. Sturgis knew that. He had to get them to an electric line soon, to recharge their woefully drained suit batteries. Or they would all freeze to death, immobilized, like some weird metal statues on the windswept Siberian plains. And America would die.

In the dim arctic half-light, in a gathering snowstorm that threatened to be yet one more obstacle to their living one day longer, they moved out, stumbling over tumuli of broken slate.

They trekked barely a mile on the frozen steppes before the colonel's helmet warning buzzer sounded. His blue-mode screen automatically had tripped the alarm. Blue for enemy approaching.

Unidentified figures—twenty six, announced the computer.

Sturgis immediately saw a number of triangles in a V pattern appear on his visor screen. "Identity?"

he asked.

Analyzing . . . Life forms . . .

While he awaited the computer's analysis, Sturgis had the men go through a weapon's systems check. They might have to drain their heat supply power entirely to power their firing modes, he realized. He hoped it was just a false alarm. That had happened before, on other missions.

Intruders identified. Species: Canis lupus.

"What the hell is a Canis lupus?" Billy asked.

Sturgis replied, "Wolves. They're nothing to worry about with our armor suits on! They're not even heading our way. They can't get our scent in these suits. Move out!"

They walked on, heading toward Yakutsk, their first expected combat stop in Russia, according to plan. Twelve miles inland, Sturgis sighted a spirelike rock outcropping and a mountain range in the distance. He stopped the column, opened the map. It was a bit soggy despite the watertight plasti-sealed bag it was in, but at least he *had* the damned thing!

After studying the map a while he said, "I think we're just about a mile off the planned route toward Yakutsk, where we all can get power recharge. There's an electric power station there—supposedly. Or there was one, before the war."

"Skip, I see blips on blue-mode again. It's the Canis lupus—all twenty-six of them," exclaimed Billy. "The tracing mode shows they're all heading right toward us."

"Skip, I thought you said they couldn't scent us," Rossiter complained.

"Maybe they saw us," Sturgis suggested. "In any

90

case, if they attack, don't waste any ammo. Smash any wolves that come close with your metal fists, or kick 'em. That should get them to lay off!"

"I sure hope so," Sheila said, "but I have a feeling. A bad one. Call it women's intuition!"

It sensed the strange things coming from the shore. Its wet black nostrils quivered and it snorted. Whatever they were, they didn't smell good; more like the noxious hard turtle things than the tasty two legged things it desired to eat. A confusion. Its keen but slow brain started working on the problem, driven by hunger. And shortly, It came up with an answer: Get closer. See more.

The Gray Leader—that's what the lead wolf would have been named if It had a name—turned, and the pack followed him up the hill. Soon they all could see the intruders. And the wolves' jaws dropped, their long sharp teeth dripping with oozed saliva. More whining, whimpering. Confusion.

The things sort of looked like moving stones. But the black things had two legs each, and shapes like the soft things that were so tasty. Conclusion: They were the food.

The pack had to have food. And Gray Leader sensed their eagerness to attack. But the pack depended on their leader to be smart. If this group of walking things smelled strange, would they taste as good as the others they had eaten? Desperate, the Gray Leader, the largest, the strongest, decided. The wolf howled the attack howl, picked up by all the rival males.

Now they ran together, excited, wild, tearing up the deep hillside snow, heading toward the black figures below. They saw the creatures stop and their strange shiny heads turn. And the Gray Leader was triumphant. For he sensed the fear.

"My God," Sturgis gasped. "Those aren't normal wolves! They're some sort of shelled things! Armadillos—or giant—somethings."

"No!" Fireheels said softly. "They're wolves all right. But they're mutations. Monster things like the walrus that killed Martinson. And there's at least two dozen of the damned things."

Sturgis shouted, "Get ready for attack . . ."

But that was a moot command. Snarling and red-eyed, drooling with unrepentant blood lust, the mutant wolves were scampering down the ridge, led by their immense gray-shelled leader. Had the world ever known greater horrors?

The humans below the wolves raised their weapon-tubes, draining all their last battery energy to power-up their firing systems. The colonel knew that they were up against the spawn of nuclear evil, horrors of the worst kind, nightmares come alive. And Sturgis knew that this attack might end their mission before it really began.

CHAPTER 13

Fenton beaded his SMG sights on the big gray wolf. But then he saw the creature turn sideways, change direction to bypass the C.A.D.S. group. Billy let loose a volley, but it bounced.

The whole wolf pack was splitting itself in half, going around, not at, the Americans.

"Bloody surprise," the Brit yelled. "They're not going to attack. And just as well; they're bloody bulletproof. Good riddance."

"No such luck, Fenton," Sturgis corrected. "They're using their brain—a strategy to come at us from all sides. Quick men, form a circle!"

"I don't like this one bit," Rossiter said. "That gray one has brain power. And we're out in the open, half of our weapons systems aborted."

"Keep tracking 'em," Sturgis ordered. "Don't lose your nerve! Everyone—activate E-ball systems, stand by."

Suddenly the mutant wolves turned and were on them.

"Fire E-ball," Sturgis ordered. Instead of a click and blast, he heard a slight beep. The words, *Aborted—jammed mechanism,* appeared on his visor screen below the wolf target.

"Shit!" Sturgis cursed. "Computer—switch to SMG mode!"

But though a withering barrage of teflon-coated explosive 9mm bullets erupted from the colonel's weapons-tube, the tremendous bony-armored gray wolf was undaunted. The slugs just bounced, exploding in the air. And the wolf reached Sturgis and knocked him over with a terrible snarling leap. No one could fire now, and not hit Sturgis, too.

The thing's double rows of acid-laden teeth snapped shut around his neckplates, and immediately the acid started dissolving Sturgis's armor. Sturgis felt the armor plate neck-ring sagging under the pressure of his attacker's teeth. Pressure on his jugular. He could hardly breathe. Still, he kicked up with all his might and the wolf was suddenly sailing free of him. The colonel rolled to the side, trying to get a bead as the giant gray-shelled post-nuke monstrosity gained its footing.

Bullets and darts flew everywhere, but the machine-gun shells and metal javelins didn't stop the armored wolves. Unless they were hit dead center in their coal-fire eyes, they just kept coming. Two men were down and the computer screen on Sturgis's suit rated them, *No life function.*

Sturgis's mind raced—what could stop such creatures? Perhaps if their E-balls could be fired— but the wolves were too mixed in with the humans. What hadn't the C.A.D.S. troopers tried yet? What can kill Goddamned lobster wolves?

Another snarling attacker leapt at Sturgis and bit into his left sleeve. The acid-laced teeth went right through the suit!

As the searing pain shot through him, the colonel reached his conclusion. "Use flame-mode," he yelled. "Steam 'em open!"

Billy wrestled free of his wolf and threw the wolf thirty feet. Then he opened up with his LPF. The searing fire blast caught the thing in midair—and a funny thing happened. The flames just burst the thing wide open. It exploded like a hot fleshy light bulb.

It fell dead, steaming, at Billy's booted feet. "The thing burst open from inside!" Billy yelled.

"Yeah, that's it! These things are like lobsters! Cook 'em like lobsters," the colonel grunted. Sturgis pried the teeth out of his arm, kicked his wolf away, and hit him with his own flame-mode. The thing, yelping in pain, burst, and then collapsed like it needed butter sauce.

"Just get them the hell away from you first—and then burn 'em," the colonel shouted. "They can't take heat."

After a while the tide of battle turned and the wolves were losing.

It, the Gray Leader, knew that the pack had lost. It ran to the side of the action and, with a howl, summoned what remained of the pack. The mournful howl pierced the cold air like a knife edge. Pointed ears stood up. Then powerful paws pushed the wolves in the direction of the timbered hills from which they had come. The gray leader knew now that the hunger, the awful hunger tearing at its guts, would go on and on. The strange human things had won.

"They've all turned tail and are heading for the woods," Rossiter exclaimed gleefully, firing a few rounds up in triumph.

"Well, I guess they learned their lesson," Sturgis intoned, "but so have we, so have we . . ."

The colonel looked around him at the carnage. The snow was spattered with red in a fifty-yard-wide circle. Blasted open steaming bony wolf shells and wolf meat trickling red were everywhere. Several of the C.A.D.S. men lay still and silent in this icy northern channel ground. He half stumbled over to a fallen trooper, tried to lift the man. The bloody helmet was split open, and coagulating blood spilled on the snow. The face plate popped off and a wide-eyed Sergeant Farrell was staring lifelessly out at black infinity, not at Sturgis.

The colonel dropped the man in the red snow and stood there gagging. There were acid holes in the man's face. The wolves' saliva was acid, which explained how they could chew metal.

"Skip," Billy reported. "Bad news. The wolves aren't moving further away. They've gathered in the treeline and they're whimpering and hollering at each other. Damn, I think they're talking to one another."

Sturgis managed to recover from his shock and

get back into the business of survival. "Well, before they can finish their next battle plan, let's wipe 'em out. We'll use the E-balls long distance—while we can. Everyone that can get his system up, fires."

"But the noise, Fenton objected. "Every Red for a hundred miles—"

"Hang the noise! We can't take another attack by those things. My E-ball system is operable on manual—how about yours, Fenton?"

"Mine will work on normal override . . ."

"Who else can fire?"

Only two other troopers' weapons tubes were functional on E-mode.

"Okay, zero in—Fenton, Tranh, Rossiter, and myself."

"Four E-balls? Skip," Rossiter asked. "Isn't that overkill?"

"You don't want to underkill, do you?"

"Okay Skip, I'm lining up," Rossiter said, in way of reply.

"Then, on my command," Sturgis ordered, gritting his teeth. "Fire all together now—E-balls spread for maximum destruction. We'll erase that whole copse of trees where they're gathered. Three . . . two . . . one . . . SINC-FIRE!"

The hellfire of the four E-balls rocketed forward. When they fell upon the pines 280 yards away, it was as if a giant meteorite had hit the earth on that very spot! The trees blew up into the air, torn like a giant's discarded toothpicks. The ice and snow melted for a hundred feet. The lobster-shelled wolves, or whatever the hell they were, were blasted to Kingdom Come.

As a billowing mushroom cloud rose on the steaming hillside, Sturgis walked around and sized up the toll. Three troopers torn to pieces, and there were two injured men, neither seriously hurt. While Sheila treated the injured for bites and acid burns, Sturgis put everyone on Red alert. He was worried that the noise—or the black cloud raised by their E-ball blasts—would attract Soviet troops.

After a while, Sheila approached Sturgis and spoke again with her visor up, rather than by radio, so the others would not hear. "Dean, I checked out the carcasses of those weird wolves we killed. They have metallike teeth and shells. They are some sort of acid-drooling mutation, like the walrus thing. I had hoped that the walrus was an isolated mutation—but now . . ."

"Yeah," Sturgis said, "I see what you mean— what's next!" A look of concern passed over his countenance.

"How's the arm the wolf bit you on, Sheila?"

"Greenwald and I patched it up, sprayed it with antibiotics. But let me know if I start scratching my neck with my feet or start howling at the moon."

He smiled at her moxie.

The C.A.D.S. team walked on silently now, Sturgis thinking, What has mankind spawned by unleashing the nukes and tampering with nature? And another thought distressed him even more. They were down by four men and hadn't even set eyes on a single Soviet soldier yet!

He thought of calling off the mission, turning back. But again the answer was—no retreat. For that would be harder than going on! So onward he led the weary nuke warriors, through the wind-driven snows of Siberia.

The temperature was minus thirty degrees. The sun was but a pale yellow smear low on the horizon. Without new power for their suits there would be another bitter cold night ahead—maybe so cold they would die.

After twenty miles, Sturgis held up his metal-gloved right hand. He heard music! Some sort of rapid playing of an unfamiliar melody, on a stringed instrument. No, several instruments!

"Fireheels," Sturgis whispered, "can you crawl up that rise and see what's making the music?"

CHAPTER 14

Joe Fireheels, A.K.A. The Invisible Warrior, was the most adept of all the C.A.D.S. troopers in infiltration, scouting and the like. Therefore, even with his armor-suit on, he disturbed not a rock on the way up the steep slope.

When he reached the summit, some thousand feet high, he reported back. "Skip, there's some sort of village below us—wooden houses, and a dilapidated church with an onion-shaped dome. There are men dancing in the square—big bearded guys. And women dancing in a circle around them. Some musicians on the side are playing triangular-bodied stringed instruments. If these guys are Russians I'll eat my helmet. They look like Genghis Khan's horde—all colorful hats and coats—lots of furs."

"Copy," Sturgis said. "Fireheels, what language are they speaking? Can you get an analysis?"

"Computer, identify language and dialect," Fireheels said.

Russian language, Uzbec tribal dialect.

"These are tribesmen, Skip. Uzbecs. Probably they're not too friendly to Moscow. The tribal groups never got along with the Communist government, for the most part."

"Now for the key question, Fireheels: Do you see any power lines in the village?"

"Yes," Fireheels said. "There's a few power lines running from the southeast right into the main house."

"Thank God! That would be the trunk line from Yakutsk," Sturgis said. "It looks like we won't have to travel any further than here to get a recharge."

There was much elation in the ranks at his words. Everyone was near freezing to death, their power down to almost nothing now.

"Are the Uzbec's armed, Fireheels? Do they have any vehicles?"

"Some horses in a corral at the edge of town, some horse-drawn sleds, Skip. I zoom-moded around the settlement. It's quite primitive. I see a few old pistols in the men's belts, and a bolt action rifle or two. As for their communications equipment—there's one line on the pole coming into town that's a phone wire, I think. That's it for this place's high tech!"

"Okay, that's good. Come back down here, Joe, before you're spotted."

As the Indian scout descended back to them, Sturgis said, "These people are not our enemies— unless they make themselves so. We will cut the phone line to make sure they don't pass on the fact that we're here, then ask for the power. If they don't give it to us, we take it anyway."

"Do we announce ourselves, Skip? I could give

'em a blast of the pipes," Fenton offered.

"Negative on the pipes, Fenton. We are going in like thieves in the night. I want a few of us at least to get full powered up before we're spotted. I also want to use some of the gold coins we brought along to buy some food—and fur outfits for us. We are heading into highly populated areas on the way to Moscow. We have to have disguises. We'll have to haul our C.A.D.S. suits, not wear them. So we need a vehicle or two, also."

DeCamp added, "Dean, we will have to bivouac here for a while. Some of the wounded need rest."

Fireheels had rejoined the troopers now, and he said, "They all seem very preoccupied with their festival or dance or whatever it is, Skip. Maybe right now is the best time to sneak into the village. I think I can lead you to the long cabin at the edge of the village without us being spotted. The power line leads right there. So does the phone line."

"Good idea, Joe. Lead on."

The weary nuke-warriors moved out in a single line, following the Indian scout.

Fireheels led them a circuitous route through the rolling hills near the town, always keeping them behind some obstacle, or behind the long wooden houses. They came to a pole with the electric and phone line on it. Billy threw a grapple line up and, snagging the phone wire, pulled it down and tore it in half.

Sturgis got a good look at the Uzbecs in the village square from the vantage point above them. What he saw was a very colorful band of joyous musicians and dancers doing a spirited *petrovska* dance. While the others waited behind a large hillside boulder, Sturgis, Billy, Wosyck, and Fireheels took advantage of the villagers' preoccupation with mirth and crossed the fifty feet of open space to the back of a rambling log house. They broke open a window. There was no shattering noise, for the window wasn't glass, but oil skin.

Inside the house they found a single large room with a few rough-hewn timber pillars. Candles set at thirty-foot intervals along the length of the hall dimly lit their way as they explored. There was a low fire burning in a large stone fireplace. There were long tables, ornately carved wooden chairs, and a beat-up metal desk with an ancient black plastic phone. Sturgis checked it by lifting the receiver. No dial tone.

"It's nice and warm in here," said Billy. Sturgis saw he had his visor up, and his metal gloves were off. He was putting his hands against the heat of the fireplace. "Can't understand why they're all out there in the cold," Billy wondered aloud. "It's warm in here!"

"This house must be their central meeting place," Sturgis said. "I doubt if the small cabins have any phones. My guess is, with this phone out, they don't have any way of contacting the outside world at all now."

"And that means," smiled Fireheels, "that we have a base of operations. Provided we can deal with the villagers."

"I found the electric outlet!" Tranh announced. "There's only one. But we can at last power up! Its two hundred and twenty volts, says the probe—

104

twice as much power as U.S. outlets."

"Great! We'll power up while they're all gathered at the town square," Sturgis called to Rossiter. "Post some of the strongest men around the town, Mickey," he radioed. "Especially along the road. I don't want any of the Uzbecs riding out of here on their horse sleighs or some hidden snow-cats."

"Right, Skip."

"Come on, Tranh. You plug in first," Sturgis commanded. "Power up to three-fourths, then Joe, Wosyck, and myself will."

CHAPTER 15

Tranh pulled his charger cord out of the left leg compartment of his suit and jammed the plug into the wall.

"Is the line taking the drain? Can it handle us?"

"Yes, thank God," Fireheels said. "I'll be charged up in five minutes."

They each took turns with the electric socket. Sturgis kept an ear out for any cessation of the festival outside, but the singing and strumming seemed to be rising in intensity, not dying out. God bless Pan, lord of mirth!

Twenty minutes later the four had a three-quarters charge in all their suit systems. All the ordinance functions were at optimum levels, too. Sturgis snapped his cord out and radioed, "Rossiter, have you covered all the exits to this town?"

"Skip, I have men at ten points in a circle around the village. If anyone tries to leave, our scanners will pick them up, and we'll stop them, one way or another."

"Okay, good work," Sturgis replied. "The four of us are going to say hello now. All troopers not engaged in the encirclement should come down into the long wooden house the same way we did now, and recharge. The outlet is on the far left wall."

Sturgis ordered the men with him to seal visors and put weapons systems on alert status, "just in case the Uzbecs don't take to us. But don't fire if they just use their old guns on us. We won't be harmed; and besides maybe a show of our invincibility will make them give us some respect."

Sturgis opened the door of the big house and stepped into the street, followed by the other three troopers. The people dancing and playing instruments in the town square one by one fell silent and turned toward them.

The women and most of the men gasped and backed slowly off toward the church step genuflecting. But the man with the big red beard made an angry gesture in the air and brazenly stepped forward. He said something loudly with a trace of a snarl in his words. Sturgis had to admire his courage. Here he was, a Siberian villager, confronted with four metal monsters with single silver eyes, and he was not withdrawing. Quite the contrary; he was shouting at them.

"What's he saying, Wosyck?"

Wosyck, the Polish-American C.A.D.S. trooper knew Russian well. The handlebar-moustached trooper translated. "Skip, this guy says his name is Zandark—the head man of this Uzbec village. He wants us 'demons' to be gone from his village or he'll throw us out."

"The guy has guts, doesn't he? Well, tell him we're friendly, but we're going to be staying for a while. Tell him we're *not* demons."

Wosyck stepped forward and raised his metal arm in the universal gesture of peace, palm forward. In Russian he rattled off: "We are men, not demons. We come in peace, and bring presents, but we must stay—"

Wosyck never finished. The Uzbec tribe leader shouted some command and then he pulled a long barreled ornate flintlock pistol from his sash belt and fired directly at Wosyck. The bullet, of course, just bounced. The other Uzbecs started throwing rocks and other objects. The C.A.D.S. men stood their ground, and Sturgis asked Wosyck what the tribes people were screaming.

"They're shouting, 'Kill the space invaders,' and 'Black Madonna preserve us, Jesus save us.' Something like that."

Someone in the back of the Uzbec crowd opened the door of the dilapidated church and the crowd, seeing that their rocks just bounced off the C.A.D.S. men, surged up the church steps and ran inside.

All except one, that is. The big fur-clad leader—Zandark—swelled his chest at them and rushed forward. The red-bearded man, snarling like a mad tiger, leapt to tackle Sturgis, actually bit at his metal arm, then howled in pain.

Sturgis shoved the man down on the packed snow. His mouth was bleeding. "That'll teach you to bite!"

Zandark spat and screamed out invectives, kicked mightily at Sturgis's metal legs.

"Shit, Skip, now what do we do?" Wosyck asked.

Sturgis hefted the big tribesman up to his feet repeating, in his halting Russian, that the man should relax, for they were humans, not space invaders.

Zandark suspiciously peered into the face plate of the colonel's helmet.

"Yes, I'm human. I am an American. From the U.S. of A. Get it? Oh, fuck this! Wosyck! Translate for me."

The Polish trooper again spat out a dozen words. This time the huge head man smiled, said something rather long and involved and, bursting with emotion, he kissed Sturgis's metal gloves. Quite an attitude reversal!

"What did he say? I didn't catch it."

Wosyck translated: "Skip, he said he loves America. He says he is Russian, but not Communist. He hates the men in the Kremlin. Any enemy of theirs is a friend of his—and so on. He wants us all to have a drink with him in the long house."

Sturgis smiled. *"Da,"* he said. "Lead on, friend."

Zandark led them back into the big house. There Fenton and a dozen others were waiting. Half the men were still in line to charge their suits from the one outlet. Zandark, saying, "American good," threw his arms around each metal-clad warrior. Then he slid a hidden panel in the wall and pulled out a dusty vodka bottle. The C.A.D.S. troopers, on Sturgis's order, opened their visors and each took a slug from the bottle to warm up. Zandark downed half a bottle on his own and passed it to Sturgis.

"Safe to take off our suits now?" Tranh asked.

"Might as well," Sturgis said. "I'll keep mine on as a precaution—you, too, Billy, Wosyck."

Zandark examined various parts of the suits, and Sturgis showed how the elbow rotated, and so on. The man's questions about the firing tube was answered by, "It's a sort of American automatic rifle."

The Uzbec chief raised his bushy red eyebrows at this and said, "Is good! Kill many Soviets!"

So the coy leader could speak English. "We fully intend to! Listen Zandark," the colonel proposed, "I want to address all your people in the church."

"Good idea," the big man said. "They should not be frightened of Americans! They should warm receive you, who we have prayed would come and free us," he bellowed.

While the other men warmed up, Sturgis and Billy went with the tribal chief back across the town square, toward the church where the villagers were holed up.

CHAPTER 16

When half the C.A.D.S. commandos strode up the snowy church steps and entered, with Zandark in front like a major domo, the hushed Uzbecs gasped and stared. Zandark smiled and told everyone not to worry, or something to that effect. Most of the Uzbecs seemed to relax a bit; but one kerchiefed-old woman, as thick as she was tall, waddled forward. She asked Sturgis who the hell they were to scare her so! Sturgis knew enough Russian—though this was an odd dialect—to understand. He said, "We are friends."

"Friends? *Bah*—look like Martians!" She spat the last word. Evidently Martians were as bad as Communists to her.

"These men *are* friends," Zandark exclaimed. "Do not be rude, old woman!" Zandark jumped up to stand on the elaborately carved pulpit. "Gentlemen, ladies," he exclaimed, "our Black Madonna, Lady of Precious Blood of Chezostowa, has brought us salvation from the Communist government at long last. May I introduce General Sturgis and the United States Army! General Sturgis, please come up here with me!"

Sturgis, somewhat taken back by the impromptu promotion to "general," pushed through the crowd and got up next to the heavy-set, bearded Uzbec leader. He spoke in halting Russian. "Friends, I am happy to bring you greetings from the president of the United States. We come to you villagers in peace, but we intend to destroy the central government. We intend to push on to the Kremlin itself and rid the world of the madman Belyakov."

Sturgis almost winced as he lay it all in the open—but there was only applause.

To a man, it appeared the Uzbecs hated the Soviet government. Everyone had been praying for years, it seemed, for the Black Madonna to send someone, anyone, to rid them of their oppressors. The women all got down on their knees and genuflected toward the altar's elaborate gold-framed icon—the Black Madonna.

The woman who had come forward earlier to criticize Sturgis now bent and kissed his boots. He was very embarrassed and tried to stop her. She was bowing and mumbling something.

"What did she say, Wosyck? I can't make it out."

Wosyck translated: "She says she knew that the Black Madonna has sent us to destroy the nonbelievers in Moscow. She says the left eye of the blessed icon picture started crying last year, around this time. The signs were all there, she says: the blood-moon on the anniversary of the October Revolution; her mare giving birth to a two-headed foal. She says

114

the Black Madonna is to end all suffering. The world is to be saved from its final days."

"I hope she's right," the colonel said softly. "It seems like we did come here at just the right time to fulfill the prophesies. But I hope the Uzbecs can give us more than applause. We need allies!"

Sturgis then got up on the dais and, with Wosyck translating, gave a speech. "Thank you for your welcome, and we'll do our best to deserve your applause in the coming days. Rest assured of that. But I want to ask you all for your help. We need food and clothing; shelter for a few days; a place to sleep. And we need your assistance in getting to Moscow, the capital of the evil Soviet Empire. Will you help us?"

There were wild cheers and promises of support. Swords and knives waved in the air. Kerchiefs waved.

"We will give you our food and lodging," Zandark promised, "and more. Your wounded will be cared for. The women of our town have marvelous folk remedies and we will fix you up. Our special energy-food is restorative. But first, you all have to kiss the blessed Madonna's icon. It is the custom."

Sturgis said, "Yes, of course we will." Wosyck looked sad as he translated. When they left the church, Sturgis was to find out why.

One by one, the C.A.D.S. men came up on the altar and bent to kiss the tip of the gold and jewel-encrusted image. Sturgis kissed the image and then watched as, one by one, the others obeyed. Wosyck, who was last in line, hesitated, his lips an inch from the image. Then Wosyck closed his eyes and kissed the icon's gold feet.

"Is good!" Zandark exclaimed. "Now we feast!"

"Yes, it's good," muttered Wosyck glumly. "May my family forgive me."

"Forgive what?" Sturgis asked.

"Forgive my kissing an *idol's* feet! I'm Jewish, and that's forbidden us!"

"Thanks, Wosyck."

"Yeah."

CHAPTER 17

Inside the "longhouse," as Zandark called the long building, the sixty-foot, rough-hewn plank table was laden with every imaginable foodstuffs from the Uzbecs' larders.

The C.A.D.S. troopers had doffed their cumbersome outfits in a corner, where they could keep an eye on them, and seated themselves along the table. Zandark was at one end and the old lady who had called them foreigners—Zandark's grandmother—was at the other end.

"There's no silverware," Billy said glumly. "Now what?"

"They evidently," Wosyck answered, "eat with their hands."

"Or," Sturgis noted, "their knives." All the Uzbecs at the table had jammed their big knives into the tabletop, to the right of their plates, he had noticed.

"So I'll eat with my bloody trail knife," Fenton grimaced. "Just so long as it's food, man. When in Rome, you know, do as the Romans. I've got to keep my bagpipe-wind in shape, you realize!"

A group of husky Uzbec women came in now, carrying huge trays of steaming sliced meat piled high as the rafters.

"Wow," Billy exclaimed, "look at that meat." He sniffed the air. "Hmmm—what is it do you suppose? Venison? Smells . . . odd."

Fenton was the fastest, jammed his knife into a morsel of meat and tasted it. He chewed and swallowed. "Very good!" he exclaimed. "Tastes like—mutton."

While all the troopers eagerly jabbed huge chunks of the repast onto their wooden plates, Wosyck asked one of the serving women what type of meat it was. She smiled a gold-toothed grin and told him. When the Polish officer heard the answer, he dropped his piece of meat on the table and turned a bit blue.

"Wosyck? Are you all right?" Sturgis asked. "What's the matter?"

Wosyck, who was seated to the left of the colonel, leaned over and said softly, "Skip, it's—wolf meat. She c-called it "Armor-wolf meat."

Sturgis looked balefully at his piled plate. "Are you sure? Do you mean that this meat is from— *them?*"

Wosyck nodded. "I'm afraid so, commander."

Sturgis sighed heavily and took the little geiger off his belt and placed it next to the plate. The meter didn't detect any radiation. He was relieved on that point, at least. Sturgis gingerly tasted it, chewed it. Soft, tender, and odd. But his stomach demanded that he swallow the juicy steaming slab of meat.

Wosyck looked at Sturgis, raised his eyebrow.

The colonel smiled. "So it's armored-wolf. The Uzbecs are eating it. It must be all right."

Wosyck nodded and started to gingerly nibble on a slice. All down the table the C.A.D.S. commandos were eagerly devouring the meat, without reservation. Sturgis decided not to tell them what it was. But the colonel's kindness was to be short-lived.

The serving women returned, rolling a huge rotisserie with trough of burning coals under it.

Billy put down his morsel and just stared. "Skip, what is that? It sort of—looks like a huge hairless gray dog—or—"

"Shit," Fenton exclaimed, "I've seen a carcass like that before! Look at the head—those horrible eyes! Why, that's a—"

"You're right," finished the colonel. "It's a mutant wolf."

"But—but we can't eat that thing," Fenton protested, looking ill.

"You have already eaten it," Wosyck said.

Fenton paled, dropped his meat-laden knife. "The bloody hell I have! You mean to tell me these Uzbec bastards—"

"It's okay." Sturgis said. "I checked the meat out for radiation. It's safe to eat, and notice how the Uzbecs are digging in."

"I'd better check the carcass out, too," said DeCamp rising. "It might be hot." She went over to the rotating spit on which the wolf-thing was being cooked, and pretended to admire how the women ladeled on grease to keep it well basted. She extracted a geiger off her belt-snap and passed the

119

rad-detection device along the carcass. "No radiation," she said, returning to the table.

"Well," Sturgis said, "what are you all looking at? Eat hearty. I thought you all were hungry. The wolves tried to eat us. And turnaround is fair play, isn't it?"

Sturgis turned to Wosyck. "Ask Zandark how the hell they catch these things without casualties."

The question was asked, the reply given. Wosyck leaned over to explain to Sturgis: "Zandark says the tribesmen dig pits, fill the pits with charcoal and heat it till there's no smoke. Then they lay wolf food out—the wolves like the entrails of goats. When the wolves come to get the goat guts, they fall into the pits and are charbroiled. He says they know the traps have worked because from the village they can hear the wolves scream, and then pop open. Zandark says the villagers, since they have been eating the shelled-wolves, have grown very strong. Not a single Uzbec, not even the old men and women, have died since they started to eat them, two years ago. That's when the wolf-things first appeared."

"Well, I hope he's right about the meat's strength building, Wosyck. A lot of our guys are weak as hell after the trek."

The troopers were served bowls of hearty meat-barley soup as dessert. It seemed like nuke wolf was the only thing on the menu except bread!

Amazingly, the flesh of the wolves immediately revitalized the weaker men. Sheila, noting their rosy-cheeked ebullience, went around and took their pulses, then reported to Sturgis. "They're recovering well from exhaustion. A good night's sleep and they'll be as good as new. I feel great, how about you? I think this wolf meat might be a tonic."

"I feel stronger, too," Sturgis admitted. "But a bit sleepy."

"Maybe it's the heat," DeCamp said, shucking her parka. "The fireplace has been piled high and roaring for an hour."

Evidently it was time for the entertainment to begin, for the headman clapped, and a company of musicians and rather full but attractive young women dancers came in. The assemblage, shorn of their heavy furs, and brightly costumed, looked a bit more Turkish than Russian. Their skins were Tartar-dark. Some of the girls and men had slightly slanty eyes, Sturgis noted.

The balalaika music began; Zandark clapped his hands again.

The Uzbec girls gave a brief, gentle, introductory dance. Then, tumbling from a side room to join the busty lasses, came twelve Uzbec men in tight red and blue patterned silk suits. Then the strangest thing happened. After the men lined up and bowed, the audience started throwing things at them! All sorts of things: saltshakers, gnawed-clean wolf bones, plates—anything at all. And the men caught the various objects and started juggling them, passing the multitudinous objects amongst one another.

"God, can you believe this?" Billy exclaimed. "They juggle everything thrown to them!"

"Oh no!" Sturgis exclaimed, as an Uzbec woman tossed her infant child, who had been at her ample breast nursing, out to the jugglers. As Sturgis winced, the juggler deftly caught the child, then passed it along down the line. The baby started giggling madly, thinking the event great fun, unaware of the danger.

"Stop!" Sturgis demanded. "Put the baby down!" But the jugglers assimilated the baby in their vast number of juggle objects. Then, other Uzbec women came from the side room and each threw their toddlers into the melange. The jugglers accommodated the five new babes, tossing them high in the air, where they were passed from one man to another, all spinning and laughing.

"I'm gonna be sick," Billy said, fearing a fatal slip of a hand.

"They haven't missed yet," Sturgis said, gripping the table edge.

The wild Steppes-music built to a crescendo, then the jugglers managed to put the children down one by one, while they threw the pieces of bone and the plates and other utensils back to the eaters. They bowed as tremendous unison clapping began. Sturgis sank back, relieved, in his seat. The mothers came forward and picked their happy children off the floor and took seats.

"Petrovshka!" Zandark shouted. "Narodysk Zimli!"

The jugglers now began to dance. At first they all danced wildly to a new, more strident accompaniment by the musicians. Then one particularly agile red-booted young man bounded forward from the other dancers who formed a semicircle. The game seemed to be for each dancer, in turn, to do a whole lot of rapid kicks from a squat position. Sturgis noted that before the second solo dancer did his bit he downed a glass full of clear liquid. It was probably vodka, not water, judging from his complexion after imbibing. Then he, too, did his magical kick-dance to the unison clapping and wild balalaika strums. One dancer after another upped the ante with wildness.

After twelve dancers had their third glass each they were even, if possible, better at the game. By the seventh glass, they were not so good, but who cared by then? Sturgis had, himself, downed a few vodkas.

"Some acrobats," Tranh said. Another of his typical understatements.

"Yeah, and the kind of acrobats we'll need when we climb the Kremlin wall," Sturgis added. "And you bet the door to the Kremlin will be closed—so we'll have to climb! I want these guys on our team."

The Uzbec chief shouted for the C.A.D.S. men to join in. Reluctant, the Americans were hustled out to join the dancers. Billy was the first to drink a glass of vodka down in two seconds, and he got out and did a strange combination of a Virginia reel and a Petrovska kicking dance. It really was something to see, and the applause was wild.

DeCamp looked over at Sturgis and said, "Come on colonel, strut your stuff—or are you chicken?"

Such a challenge could not, Sturgis realized, be ignored.

"I'll have a go," he said. Sturgis threw some vodka down and started to do a deft-footed dance, more closely resembling the Uzbec dance than Billy's. He felt loose and strong—and happy.

The Uzbecs went mad with pleasure at the

C.A.D.S. men's eagerness to join them. Wosyck was next, and proved to be a pretty good stepper. He did the Polish version of the Russian dance, which had a few more swirls and spins to add to the kicks, and he insisted on having a woman to dance with him. Sheila DeCamp!

Sheila gamely tried the dance for a while, then stood up and downed a vodka, leaving Wosyck to his own devices. She grabbed Sturgis from the onlookers and yelled, "Do you know any Chuck Berry?" at the musicians. One of the men with an oversized twelve-string lute shouted back, "Chuck Berrysky? *Da! Da!*" And he rapidly fired off instructions to the other five players. Quickly the beat changed to a four-beat rock-and-roll, "Johnny B. Goode."

Sheila got Sturgis into a careening version of the lindy, but then the music speeded up, faster and faster. People kept shoving full glasses of vodka into Sturgis's hand as he danced, and he kept handing them back—or drinking and throwing them into the fireplace—empty. Soon he was dead drunk on his feet.

Chuck Berrysky went on and on. Soon everyone started jitterbugging to the wild Russian-distorted beat, even the Uzbecs. The C.A.D.S. men selected partners from the Uzbec women and tried to teach them some American freestyle. To Sturgis, the room started to blur and spin, even when he stopped dancing. He thought he heard bagpipes—and he later recalled dimly seeing Fenton running around in his jockey shorts blowing on his sadly mistuned and warped instrument. He later also remembered saying to Sheila, "I feel sick." He also remembered staggering over to a corner and leaning against the wall.

Indeed, one by one, all the C.A.D.S. troopers fell by the wayside. But only now had Zandark consumed enough vodka to dance. He started heaving his massive frame around, but not on the floor: rather on top of the table, scattering glasses and plates as he tripped and swirled down the length of the table. His huge feet demolished every single bit of crockery they had eaten upon, saving endless dishwashing.

Sturgis remembered Zandark falling off the table and rolling to lie at his outstretched feet. Then he remembered nothing at all.

CHAPTER 18

The colonel woke up when the door of the small cabin, in which he was lying on a cot, opened. Brilliant sunlight glared off some hanging icicles on the doorframe and into his puffy eyes. He groaned and yelled, "Shut the door." His head hurt with every word he uttered. Never had he such a hangover in his whole life! He moaned, "Ohhhh . . ." Then he tried to get a hold of the bed, to keep it from spinning, and somehow got up stiffly.

Sheila came to his aid and helped him stand up. She handed him something like black mud—Russian coffee. "Here, have some wake-up tonic." He started to say something but his head hurt too much to continue. Each word pounded like an Uzbec dancer's boot.

He fell asleep again despite the coffee and slept most of the day. Sturgis awoke much later and found some of the other men—puffy red-eyed to a man—were sitting around his bed.

"Good afternoon," Billy said.

"Afternoon?"

"Yes, it's three P.M.," said Tranh.

"Here, have some hair of the dog that bit you," Fenton offered, handing him a full water glass of clear death.

"More vodka? You gotta be kidding!" Sturgis exclaimed, pushing the glass away.

"Just a little more of the same is the best thing for a hangover," the Brit insisted.

The colonel adamantly refused and eventually he was handed a cup of coffee, which he imbibed in huge gulps.

The door again opened and let in painful bright Arctic sunlight. Chief Zandark said, "Is good sunny day, General Sturgis." Sturgis and the chief, with Wosyck translating what the colonel couldn't catch of the chief's dialect, got down—over yet more coffee—to negotiating an agreement. Zandark was eager to help the C.A.D.S. men, whom he called "great party animals." In exchange for half the gold U.S. coins Sturgis had along, Zandark said he would supply all their needs for the journey to Moscow. That included clothing and horses—and a covered horse-drawn sled for the C.A.D.S. suits. Plus ten Uzbec men, the best acrobats from the dance the night before.

The plan was to get to Marinsk, a big, poorly guarded truck facility and steal some trucks.

"It is circus season hereabouts," Zandark explained. "Caravans of entertainers make way from small towns like this to remote Soviet garrisons—entertain soldiers there. We will be able get right into the base without fighting, if we look like *be*

128

such entertainers."

"Great," Sturgis said, "I was hoping you'd come up with some idea on how we could get mechanized transport. Horses and sleds won't do for getting to the Kremlin."

Just then the door burst open. It was a committee of six surly-looking Uzbecs.

"Rivals to the chieftain," Wosyck explained. They were headed by a short wide man with two gold front teeth. His name is Amarr, he said loudly. Then Amarr growled out, "I believe that the C.A.D.S. soldiers are shams. That their clumsy metal suits have no power. It is just to keep these American weaklings warm. Why should we follow people to Moscow who have to wear spacesuits to survive in normal weather? How can we trust our lives with these Americans? The Soviets will punish us when the Americans are destroyed."

Zandark pushed the squat man back. "Amarr—the Americans are powerful!"

"How do we know?" Amarr said. He spoke English very well.

"I say so, that is why!" the chieftain exclaimed, his eyes narrowing into slits. *Do you call liar me?*

Now Amarr backed down a bit. "I—and many others—just want to have the Americans prove the power they boast of. They have bragged that they have the power to wreck the Kremlin! If their metal suits have such power, let them show us that power. Only then should we help them!"

There were several grunts of approval of Amarr's statements from the other intruders. Zandark gave them the fish-eye.

"Wosyck, tell this guy Amarr that I don't want to waste ammunition," Sturgis protested. "We don't have time for games."

"No need translate," Amarr said in British-accented English. "I study English for years. I listen to BBC and Voice Of America! No excuse! Show us power!"

Sturgis frowned. "Very well, Amarr. We'll show you firepower. Gentlemen—let's all retire to the south end of the village . . ." He took one more slug of black coffee, donned a parka; then they all followed the C.A.D.S. leader out the door.

Gathered at the edge of town, the C.A.D.S. men, all in their armor-suits, stood at attention and watched as their commander Dean Sturgis spoke to Amarr. They saw Sturgis point his weapons-arm at a fifty-foot-high bronze statue on a concrete pedestal.

"See that statue of Stalin? You wouldn't miss it, would you?"

"Not one bit," Amarr snorted. "Up until Great Nuke War, we think best to leave up, to pretend loyalty to Belyakov. His people built it when they took over from Gorbachev peace party. They like Stalin, put up statues of the butcher everywhere! We villagers spit on statue every time we pass."

"Well then," the C.A.D.S. commander said, "it's time to get rid of it, don't you think?"

"We will pull it down soon, with block and tackle," Zandark grunted out.

"Why wait when you can do this," Sturgis said. "Computer, lock onto target oh-three-oh degrees."

"Locked." Dean felt the chunk, the weighty shell locking into place under his sleeve.

He pointed his arm at the statue—midway up. "Everyone get back a hundred feet. Better make that two hundred. Get behind some cover in case fragments come your way."

"Bah," Amarr scoffed. "What is he going to do with his silly metal suit?" Still, he judged discretion the better part of valor, and backed off ten paces. So did the other villagers.

"Fire E-ball," Sturgis shouted. The E-ball rocketed forth from his weapons-tube, straight at the bronze madman. The shimmering electro-ball shell hit the midsection of old Uncle Joe Stalin, and the feet-thick bronze metal blew apart into small, ultrahot fragments of molten dust and rock. The E-balls concussion knocked Amarr's men off their feet. They scrambled upright and, like the other villagers, took off in the opposite direction from the toppling remains of Butcher-Joe's head and neck.

When they came out from their hiding, Sturgis lifted Amarr by his greasy lapels high over his head and said, "So now you see the power of our weapons!"

Amarr nodded vociferously. "Yes! Yes! No harm intended. I just wanted to *know*."

Sturgis spent the whole day selecting the Uzbec men who would make the journey with them. Zandark insisted he go along to lead the Uzbec volunteers, and Sturgis agreed. The colonel wouldn't have expected the Uzbecs to follow his orders anyway.

He picked out five of the juggler/dancers and asked Zandark for some crack shots.

"Mordark, Weromak," Zandark ordered. "Come over here."

Two strapping blond-haired youths—one with just the faintest trace of a beard but lanky and muscular—eager to prove himself, stepped up. "I kill bear one hundred meters!"

Soon there were seventeen Uzbecs coming along plus Zandark. Good enough, but Sturgis had an idea. Call it a hunch. He asked Amarr, who was standing behind the volunteers sulking, to join them on the mission.

He was all smiles and eager to go, and grateful.

"Well, that's it then," the commander said. "Now for supplies."

"It is near sunset," the chieftain said. "You have done enough, General Sturgis. Your assistants can handle supplies. It is time, General Sturgis, for you to sleep!"

Sturgis admitted it; he was exhausted. Last night's hangover-recovery sleep had hardly been enough.

CHAPTER 19

Sturgis summoned Billy and Tranh, who had been resting, and they took over. He went off to his cabin, shucked his gear and fell into bed, asleep before he hit the sheets.

Sheila was already at the breakfast table with Billy and Fireheels when Sturgis sauntered in, well rested and newly showered and shaved. "How do you like my Uzbec sealskin parka and boots?"

"Well, here's the sleepyhead," she snorted. "No thanks to you I still have my virginity. Screw your fashion show!"

"What do you mean?"

"I mean, if you were sleeping in my cabin, I wouldn't have had to fend off these damned amorous Uzbec men all night!" She flushed red.

"Are you okay?"

"Sure—but I had to put the chair under the door, and even then, they sang to me all night!"

Sturgis smiled and poured himself some coffee. "Sorry, Sheila. It's the wolf meat, probably. It makes them wolves!"

"Yeah sure."

Billy cut in: "Aw—quit griping, DeCamp—it all worked out okay. Here, have some more of these wolf-meat flapjacks!"

"Sturgis groaned. "More wolf stuff?"

"No. There's also some barley porridge, if you want," Fireheels said. "But these wolf-based foods are good for what ails the men, Skip. I, for one, feel like a sixteen-year-old!"

"Well!" Sheila frowned, putting down her fork. "I suppose nobody *cares* that I nearly got raped last night. Least of all our colonel!"

"Women," said Billy, after she slammed the door. He poured himself some coffee and added caribou cream. "You can't figure 'em, can you, Skip?"

"I suppose they did give her a fright," Sturgis said. "I guess I didn't treat what she said very seriously. I'll talk to her later." The colonel changed the subject. "Say, Billy, you look rather pleased with yourself this morning. What gives?"

The Southerner gave a half-smile. "Didn't I mention? Ilyana, the younger sister of Amarr, and I had a little snuggle session. *Man,* that wolf meat put the wolf in me, I'll tell you! We went at it all night!"

"You devil you," Sturgis grinned. "We've got to bring that wolf stew on the mission. Or at least some broth. Make a note to fill a few canteens with it."

In the bright noonday sun, the Uzbecs cheered

and made way as the C.A.D.S. soldiers and the tribe's volunteers walked across the town square toward the corral at the east side of town.

At the corral, the C.A.D.S. officers and men got a chance to see close up the beautiful, rugged short ponys of the wild Steppes tribesmen. The Uzbec horses looked back at them, staring.

Sturgis looked dubiously into the angry eyes of one palomino pony. "I don't think this one likes me. But where's the saddle? I'll give it a try. He sure looks strong enough to carry me."

"Coming up," Zandark said.

Sturgis found the saddle very hard and thin. Zandark, seeing his frown, slapped him on the back and rattled off something that the colonel didn't catch. "What did he say, Wosyck?"

"He said," Wosyck translated, "you don't have to use a saddle. Zandark doesn't."

Sturgis and the others saddled and bridled the horses.

"Well, here goes! Let's mount up. You too, Billy."

"I can't believe I'm doing this," Billy exclaimed as he mounted his whinnying beast. His horse, at least, stayed put. Sturgis got up on his mount next. The horse bucked for a while, but settled down fast, when Amarr threatened it with a tree limb.

"Well, that's better! Now if they follow orders," Sturgis said, " we can get to our next stop."

"It's easy, Skip. Pull left to go left and . . ."

"Very funny, Billy," Sturgis sniffed. His mount reared just then and he had a devil of a time controlling it. Still, in a half hour, they all had gotten the hang of it, by practice-riding a few times around the two hundred foot circular enclosure of the corral.

The weather was sunny and it was ten degrees. The horsemen all lined up to leave the village. On Sturgis's order, they rode out, their horses laden with Uzbec-supplied foodstuffs and small amounts of ammo. Billy and Fenton each drove the two-horse, covered sleighs. Both sleighs were filled with the C.A.D.S. suits. Tranh and Rossiter rode shotgun to the suits inside the closed sleighs, remaining in their armor—just in case of sudden need.

Sturgis didn't envision going all the way to Moscow as a traveling circus—that was what the sled-wagon's tarpaulin covers said they were. They were headed to Marinsk, the nearest Soviet garrison. Heading at last to a confrontation with the Sovs. They would procure some faster transport and better arms at that isolated truck depot—by force!

CHAPTER 20

Sturgis and his nuke troops, clad in furs and embroidered sealskins and silks, looked like a horde of Tribal horsemen. They were all bearded, thanks to some borrowing of hair for false beards. Now at dusk, they came riding down out of the snowy hills toward Marinsk followed by two circus sleighs. Sturgis felt confident, buoyed even. Brazenly, the entourage made no attempt to hide. They were, after all, supposedly traveling entertainers. Entertainers who would be most welcome in this cold bleak season. The isolated garrison of Soviet forces at Marinsk would welcome them with open arms.

At six P.M. local time, the riders were on the ridge overlooking the base. Fireheels said, "This looks like a pushover, Skip. The whole base is actually just three log cabins. Look at all those trucks! Must be a hundred of 'em, just sitting there, waiting for us to pick and choose."

"Yeah," Sturgis said, "but why are all the motors of those trucks running? You can tell that by the exhaust smoke."

Amarr said, "The trucks have to be kept running all winter, or they'll never start. Don't worry, we are aware that there are only a handful of soldiers here, just enough for fueling the trucks from cans, and making sure they don't stall. You see, the trucks will be used starting next month in the Trenkov salt fields."

Zandark explained: "A new shipment of dissidents is soon arrive; work mines."

"What happened to the old dissidents?"

"The last shipment of prisoners has been worked to death," Amarr said.

"That's a pretty smooth highway. How do you suppose they maintain it?" asked Billy, turning to the red-bearded headman.

Zandark laughed. "That is frozen river! No road! Is best roads of Russian winter all big rivers! They are much solid from September through May!" He laughed heartily. "Cold *good!*"

"They must have quite a job keeping the trucks fueled," Billy reasoned, "and I'll bet some nights they don't want to come out in the cold and do their job."

"Enough," Sturgis said, irritated. "No more talking. Let's get down where they can see us. I caught the glint of a binocular lens in the window of the middle cabin."

The "circus" started descending the hill, making as much noise as possible. The balalaikas and bagpipes of the circus made an odd combination, Sturgis thought. A fitting sort of calliope sound. Especially the warped balalaika played by Billy, who

138

knew only the banjo. The bagpipe was the one that Fenton had rescued from its sodden state: with some caribou skin patches to make it function, it was earsplitting.

"God, that sounds weird," Wosyck said. "Hurts my ears."

"Mine, too," said Sturgis, "but we have to show we're not sneaking up on them. That's the point. Keep your weapons out of sight," Sturgis added. He had a small communicator button in his ear, and thus the colonel could speak to the two fully equipped C.A.D.S. troopers in the wagons. "If there's any firing at us—wipe the mothers off the damned ice, got that?" he ordered.

"Got you, Skip," Rossiter said.

"Copy," Tranh acknowledged tersely.

They rode down the hill as a dozen blue nylon parka-clad Red soldiers exited the log cabins to watch the weird entourage arrive. The soldiers were joking among themselves and their rifles remained on their backs. Evidently they suspected nothing. Sturgis's keen eyes swept the scene. "Just a little bit closer men, that's it. Rossiter, can you target them all with just your LPF-mode?"

"Yeah, they're bunched up real nice."

"Tranh, get ready to jet-pack through the cabin windows and mess up the interiors of those huts."

"They're probably all out here, my sensor probes indicate . . ."

"Just in case your sensors are wrong. It happens. Waste the interiors!"

"Okay."

Sturgis tensed up and in a low voice said,

"Ready . . . on the count of three. One . . . two . . . *three!*"

Fenton pulled the pipe out of his mouth and his instrument emitted a dying mournful sound. Then he showed what was under this Brit's kilt: *an SMG.* The other riders dropped their Russian string instruments in the snow and leveled the hodgepodge of pump-shotguns, old revolvers, even flintlocks, that the Uzbecs had armed them with. It was a staccato, smoky barrage they fired at the surprised Sovs, but effective. Before the dozen sloppy outpost troops could respond, they were set afire by a wide swatch of liquid plastic fire, or cut down by rusty Uzbec bullets.

Tranh jumped from his hiding place and jet-pack cannon-balled himself through the central cabin's window, smashing it to hell. A few screams and blasts proved to Sturgis that there were more Reds inside the building. Temporarily. The ones that Tranh missed were burned down in their skivvies by Rossiter, waiting outside. The other cabins were broken into, but all the attack-teams found were supplies of blankets and bedding.

"We can use these blankets," Fireheels said, "to sleep in the trucks on the way to Moscow."

"Yeah," Billy sneered, "they won't need 'em."

The American-Uzbec team, Sturgis realized, just had their first triumph.

He cut short their shouts of jubilation with sharp orders: "Barclay," Sturgis said. "Shoot your injured horse! Zandark! Could you send one man back to the village with the rest of our mounts? We're traveling first class from here on! Men, round up any shells that will fit our V.S.R. mechanisms and load them into your suits. Then pile what you find of SMGs and ammo in—let's see—those three new trucks in the second row. Then, we'll get the hell out of here and on to Moscow! Oh—bring the blankets!"

There were a few more cheers from the victors, but they moved to action. They quickly did what their commander asked and Zandark ordered Belosh, an Uzbec who had been wounded in the arm in the firefight, to take the horses and sled wagons back to the village. "Tell them we were successful at Marinsk and are on our way."

"I am sorry I don't go on with you," Belosh said, "but without my shooting arm, I am useless. It is best," he agreed sadly, "that I do this duty."

Sturgis said, "DeCamp, give him some treatment for that arm. And enough antibiotics so it doesn't get infected."

DeCamp tore the wounded Uzbec's bearskin sleeve to expose the wound and announced, "It's not too bad. I can do a patch job." She dug out the bullet—the Uzbec proudly stifling his scream and refusing anesthetics. She gave him the steel slug. "Now," she said, "if you eat some of that wolf soup when you get back home, you should be fine!"

Belosh gave her a big Russian bear hug, tempered by his sore arm, and a wet kiss. He got on his horse and rode back toward the village, the other horses gladly following of their own accord. He left the beat-up old sled, which still had to be unloaded into the commandeered trucks.

Sturgis and the others filled the three best trucks

with full tanks of gas and put many cans of gasoline in the back as well. They loaded in their C.A.D.S. suits and ammo and roared off down the frozen river highway, heading for Moscow, capital of the Evil Empire.

"Geez, I hope the river ice holds," Billy muttered under his breath. "These trucks are heavy, aren't they?"

Sturgis said, "Russians do this all the time. Don't worry." But he was a bit worried. C.A.D.S. suits were heavy.

They drove on and on for two days, relieving one another as drivers; those not driving or riding shotgun were playing cards in the back of the trucks or sleeping there. Their departure had been hasty, so they went over some of the supplies in the stolen trucks as they drove—and found vodka, whips, chains—and toilet paper. Plus cans of rations— pork belly hash and thousands of cans of Diet Pepsi in a special no-freeze compartment.

"Great, we can wipe our ass, whip the peasants, and slim down," Fenton lamented. They chucked some of it to get more room.

Sturgis was pleased to find that all the trucks had simple, clear intercoms mounted on the dashboards. This allowed each truck's occupants to clearly hear what was being said in the other vehicles.

It was smooth going at first. Then, on the third day the riverbed cut into a canal. The canal was also, judging by the tracks of vehicles Sturgis spied on the ice, used as a roadway. Recently. Sturgis was at the wheel of the lead truck. He tried to make speed but suddenly hit the brakes and shouted, "Trucks ahead!"

Amarr, who was riding shotgun alongside Sturgis, said, "Is okay! Just join them. Trucks often travel together, so if a truck stall it have help. Many driver dies if he is not noticed out here. They will not question us!"

Sturgis said, "I hope you're right." He closed up the distance between him and the last slow truck of the big convoy ahead. Nobody said anything or did anything, but everyone was feeling very tense. There were a hell of a lot of Russians with them now! Still, they were not challenged.

Another ten hours and they passed a signpost: Moscow Five Hundred Km. That was a long way at thirty kilometers per hour.

Sixteen hours later they saw onion-domed buildings and some spired skyscrapers. They were, Sturgis realized, now on the outskirts of the fabled Moscow, City of Death.

"Those buildings look like wedding cakes," Billy said.

"Don't think much of the architecture," sniffed Rossiter on the com. "I like Frank Lloyd Wright's buildings better."

"I don't know." Sturgis paused. "It's kind of pretty."

"Never thought I'd be visiting here," Billy said. "When I was a boy in the South, never thought I'd get east of Atlanta!"

"Fickle finger of Fate," Fenton quipped.

CHAPTER 21

Ilya Demski stood and adjusted his striped tie in the full-length mirror. This mirror, like all the furnishings, were recent acquisitions. Star quality. That's what he was. Important. Ever since Menshekov had taken the reigns of government from Premier Belyakov, Demski's stock had risen.

Now he and his wife, and other Menshekov supporters, were to be personally honored. They were invited to the hottest ticket concert in years—at the Bolshoi Theater.

The gentleman's gentleman he had hired—Boris —put on another of his many military decorations. "Don't forget my Cross of Lenin," Demski said, "for shooting down the American bomber on N-day."

"Of course, Your Excellency," the very classy butler smugly replied. "You must be completely fitted out just perfect for tonight's celebration."

"Svetlana," Demski called out. "Oh where is that woman?"

"Here I am, dear." She was dressed in a royal blue

sequined evening gown, an exact copy of the last czarina's, the bodice pushing up her ample breasts so that you could almost see the nipples.

Ilya Sebastian's mouth watered. She was so beautiful. And now she had what she deserved. He was no longer a minor bureaucrat in the transportation department. He was to be promoted—honored tonight. Who knew what rank he would be tomorrow? She would be the wife of someone famous.

"Dear, the children were just on the phone. They send their best wishes for you."

Demski smiled. Little Andrei and little Ninotchka, five and six years old, were at the Music Training Institute outside of Moscow, a wonderful place. They were getting a fine elite education—and keeping out of his hair as well.

The door burst open and the doorman said, "The limousine is waiting downstairs, master—the one to take you to the Bolshoi Theater."

"Tell them to cool their heels for a minute. I will be down. Hurry up, Boris! Forget the riflery metals."

"Yes sir! There." Boris combed Demski's hair a bit down and sprayed it.

"You look stunning, darling," Svetlana said and hugged him.

"Careful. Don't crease my uniform." He put on the white gloves and, arm in arm, they walked downstairs and got in the giant limousine idling at the curb.

The theater was partly filled. The doors sealed shut, the red-clad ushers locking them.

"Why are they being locked?" Ilya asked in a whisper.

Svetlana smiled. "Probably to prevent gate crashers. Hold my seat dear." Her face quivered slightly.

"What's the matter?"

"Nothing. Just have to make a trip to the restroom. It's that time of month."

"Hurry back." He watched the curtain. Sometimes there were figures bumping it from behind. He couldn't wait. They had been promised the greatest surprise show ever arranged.

The curtain rose. And the audience faced a phalanx. Two rows of rifle-holding troops. The rifles were pointed at the audience. Not much of a backdrop, he thought. Grim pockmarked walls, Pollocklike splashes of blood, broken pianos. Dismal, as a matter of fact. Was this some sort of war drama? He much preferred muscials. Then the spots of red came on.

What was swinging in the air? God! Dripping pieces of—looked like human bodies—legs and arms and severed heads.

God, this wasn't fun at all. Too real! And the orchestra, where was the orchestra? The pit was empty save for instrument cases. The audience, including Demski, rustled uncomfortably in their seats.

General Dimitrov, a loyal supporter of Belyakov, the deposed premier, stepped out, his jackboots clicking across the stage. He pulled his saber. A roar went through the audience. "What is Dimitrov doing here? Wasn't he purged—*dead?*" They shouted.

147

"Ready," said Dimitrov. The rifles safeties clicked off. "Aim . . ."

"Aim? What the hell is—" Demski leapt from his seat—"going on?"

"Fire!" A massive volley of bullets hurtled at the audience. The man in front, and another to the side of Demski; chests burst open and they fell, spurting blood, on the floor.

"Reload," the man on stage said, "and fire at will."

There was a general panic. Screaming patrons stumbled over bodies. Demski found an opening, plunged into the orchestra pit, and hid behind the cello case, opening the cover. He couldn't quite get in. The irregular firing continued for some time. The smell of cordite in the darkness. Then he heard soldiers saying, "This one's dead. This one, too." Occasionally a coup de grace shot.

His heart pounded—and Svetlana, what of her? Had she managed—

The cello case was pushed aside. He stared at Dimitrov.

"Ah, Demski! We meet again. Remember when you had me jailed for smoking in the Presidium?" He smiled. "Now it is I who arrest you! In the name of state security, you are under arrest!"

"Why? Who put you in charge?" Demski screeched. "Why this slaughter? I support new Premier Menshekov. Why arrest me? Kill these others, but not me! I am a hero. I and my air squadron helped defend Moscow from Stealth bombers—successfully. I am a hero! I am in all the history books."

Dimitrov smirked. "You are historically *irrelevent*—like Gorbachev—like Trotsky! You and your

148

children will be erased. There will be no trace, even in books. You will be removed out of the pictures you mention. You will never have existed."

"But why?"

"Because, you see, Belyakov is still in power." He smirked.

Demski paled. "The coup wasn't real? Menshekov isn't in charge?" His lips got too dry. "Then—it is a trick?"

"Exactly. To flush out his enemies—you were one of the first to lavish praise on Menshekov, and expose your past scheming and dealings with him—so . . ."

There was nothing to do now except—Demski, with a smile of partial triumph on his lips, reached for the Tokarev pistol under his jacket saying, "At least *you* won't live to gloat, bastard! And he fired. Click. Click-click click!

"No bullets? How?" Demski stared at his empty Tokarev.

Dimitrov snapped his fingers. Demski's wife Svetlana came from the stage, down the staircase to the pit. "Yes," she said. "It is empty. I emptied the gun yesterday."

"But all those years—were you—with them?"

"You were right. I *was* too beautiful to love a pig like you."

"But the children?"

She regarded him coolly. "I am a tool of the state. I gave you children—but all the time I was a member of KGB, and I denounce you now!"

"I see." His heart was broken. "But they will kill *you*. Belyakov's policy is to kill the children of traitors; and wives too."

"No, we won't kill her," said Dimitrov. "She has proved ultimate loyalty to the state. And she is good breeding stock—proven nonradioactive; no gene problems. As for the children . . ."

Svetlana shouted. "But you cannot kill my children. I could not stand that. Shoot me now!"

"You will never remember them," Dimitrov smiled. "You will continue to serve the KGB. We will erase your memory, Svetlana; you understand that! Give you a new husband. It is painless—some drugs, a few months reeducation. You will be a new Soviet woman."

She said, "I have no choice. I do what is right for the state. That is my duty."

"Good. I am glad that your loyalties are clear—but to prove it . . ." Dimitrov handed her the gun. "You shoot him. Shoot Ilya!"

She aimed correctly and almost a whole clip of bullets entered his stomach before he knew it. And Demski's last vision was Svetlana's smile growing dark.

"Svetlana, do not concern yourself with the funeral—we have arranged it. A pit behind the building filled with lime. Now, you must go to the institute for retraining."

She shuddered. Was it so simple to replace her memories? Svetlana had heard rumors that the methods weren't painless drugs, but rather behavior-modification by pain and more pain; until they hold up their five fingers and say four and you see four fingers!

There was one bullet left. She used it on herself.

CHAPTER 22

The Tech Commandos drove very close behind the convoy into the City of Evil. Ahead was the biggest challenge so far to the success of the mission: The main Moscow Checkpoint. Wosyck was at the wheel next to Sturgis, who rode alongside in the truck's cab. He had a confiscated Kalashnikov SMG on his lap, safety off. They would have to bluff their way through.

"If there's a problem, Wosyck, put the pedal to the metal," Sturgis grimaced.

One by one, the trucks ahead showed their papers and were waved on by the two burly guards. Now it was Wosyck who rolled open his window and pulled up to the barrier.

"Where's papers?" asked the shorter guard as the other leveled his SMG at Wosyck. Sturgis was glad Wosyck's Russian was perfect.

Wosyck said, "The truck ahead had my papers! He has the papers for the last three trucks; didn't he show you?"

The guard looked suspicious and leaned a bit to look at Sturgis. Wosyck continued on in rapid Russian. "Comrades! What's the problem? It's freezing out. Go back inside—here, take these!" Wosyck picked two vodka bottles off the seat and handed one to each soldier. "Here, enjoy yourselves. *Da?*"

"Da." They smiled, going off with the booze. "No problem!"

The barrier went up.

"Good thing they like vodka so much," Sturgis said, "or they'd be dead men now."

"Yeah," replied the Pole, "and so would we."

They went down the last stretch of road before the highway dissipated into the city. Sturgis gasped, for all along the avenue they drove down he saw frozen naked bodies hung, nailed to wooden crucifixes.

"Stop here; pull over," Sturgis said. "Let's find out what gives." Sturgis got out and went up to a solitary man praying in front of one cross. He was knees-down in six inches of cold snow.

"What's happening here, comrade," Sturgis asked in his best Russian. "Why are all these—things— here?"

"You must be from far away," the old man said. "There is a purge going on now—the worst ever! Glad to hear, though, that the bastard who started the war is dead!"

"Belyakov's dead?" gasped Sturgis. "Then who's the premier now?"

"Let's see," said the old man. "I know I can remember the name . . . Tokaminsk . . . no, Mertanov . . . no . . . Let's see . . . *Ah!* The new premier is Sergei Menshekov! He is a peaceful man, I hear, though this isn't very evident yet, as you can see. As a matter of fact, events are quite confusing! For instance, stranger, these men on the crosses—many of them are Menshekov supporters—or were! Maybe they betrayed him; that must be why they are nailed up like this."

Sturgis asked, "Why are you praying for this man? Is he a particular friend of yours?"

"Oh no, stranger," the man smiled toothlessly. "You see, it's my *job*. The glorious communist state makes sure everyone has a job. My mother, she sells ice cream in Red Square at this moment. And I am employed as a state mourner. I spend five minutes per crucifixion."

"I understand," Sturgis said, not understanding at all. "Er—isn't it a bit cold to sell ice cream?"

"Momma doesn't sell that many, that is true, stranger. But at least it doesn't melt!"

Sturgis got back in the truck, waved the other two trucks behind them to again follow. Wosyck put the Misha in gear and moved on. "Where we headed, colonel?"

"Into the heart of the beast," Sturgis replied, "to cut it out."

Soon they saw shop windows laden with lots of items—from watches to dressing gowns—things stolen, no doubt, from all over the world. One store, and one alone, had a line of people in front of it.

"What's the line for? Can you read the sign, Wosyck?"

"Yes. It's a line for—toilet paper!"

"You're kidding!"

"Serious, Skip," the Pole said, scratching at his thick moustache.

"Hey, don't we have lots of that in the back of this truck?" Sturgis said. "That big carton?"

Wosyck said, "Yes, I think so!" He pulled the truck over.

"Back up," Sturgis said. "I'm getting out again."

"Man, you can't do that. There are soldiers guarding that line, to make sure no one cuts in. What do you want to stop for, colonel? You're not thinking of talking to the soldiers!"

"We're short of ammo—the small-caliber stuff like rifle bullets."

Wosyck paled. "Oh no! You're not planning to trade the soldiers toilet paper for bullets!"

"Oh yes! And I need your fluid tongue. Come on, Wosyck!"

The men in the back of the truck passed Sturgis the carton of twelve dozen rolls of toilet tissue. He and Wosyck hefted it over to the line. Eyes lit up like pinball stations when the Soviets realized what they were carrying.

It took guts, but Wosyck helped trade their toilet paper shipment for twelve hundred bullets—emptied from the Soviet soldiers' rifles! They filled a gunnysack with the ammo and then they climbed back in the lead truck. "Okay—it's on to the Kremlin," Sturgis said, exultantly. "I feel better now that we can shoot at the Reds instead of wiping their asses!"

"Er, Skip, we did save *some* of the toilet paper, didn't we?" Wosyck asked. "That deal back there—kinda . . ."

"Oh shit! I forgot!" Everyone had a laugh at that remark.

Sturgis consulted the street map on his lap. "Turn left here. Now we need a secure base of operations. A place to plan, get into out suits, the whole bit. And as near to the Kremlin as possible. Any suggestions, men?"

At that moment they were entering Red Square itself. They slowed down and rolled past the squat bare black marble building marked in Cyrillic, Lenin Tomb.

"Skip," Billy said. "Lenin's tomb is really close to the Kremlin's wall. And there's only those two goose-stepping guards with decorative rifles. I bet they don't even have bullets!"

"Yeah, I get it, Billy, but that's a crazy idea!"

"Still," said Tranh, "I think he's on to something. It would be a great base of operations, and very unexpected!"

"Well, that's it then," Sturgis said. "Slow down, Wosyck. Let's check this out! We're on a roll, don't you think?"

The trucks ground to a halt in the six-inch-deep snow. Sturgis took up the binocs. "There's no line of visitors in front of the tomb. In the pictures I've seen, there's always a line to get in to see the big man's body!"

Zandark's voice crackled over the radio from the second truck. He remarked, "Bah—no one go there anymore. The body is in terrible shape. I am told Lenin *smells!*"

"Skip," Mickey said, "those goose-stepping guards probably have an office in there and if that's so, there might be relief men. Another shift of guards maybe. So, expect at least four guards."

"Big fuckin' deal," Billy countered. "We can handle them. They ain't expecting nothing!"

"And if our men replace the guards we knock out," Sturgis said, "no one will be the wiser."

Zandark cut in: "There is rumor that tunnels reach from tomb right under Kremlin. I have brought the old map that shows!"

"I like it," Sturgis decided. "Taking the tomb as a base is bold as hell. And who knows; there may be something to this tomb-tunnel legend."

"Yes, czarist tunnel is just under tomb," Amarr said. "We can burrow in and have a shortcut. No need to climb walls!"

"The C.A.D.S. troopers pulled their trucks over just behind the tomb. The two elite guards didn't give them a glance as the attackers got out and milled around smoking cigarettes. They acted like cold, tired, long-haul drivers—rubbing their hands, taking a leak on the tires. Billy lifted the engine cover of one truck, feigning mechanical difficulties. A light snow was falling.

The routine parading over, the guards were about to goose-step back into the tomb. They never made it. Billy and Sturgis grabbed and garroted them. The C.A.D.S. troopers quickly rushed in, shot the two relief guards who were lifting their guns too late. The Americans piled the four bodies to the side.

156

"Easy as pie," Sturgis said. "Let's search the place."

Their bootsteps echoed in the bare mausoleum. There weren't any other guards inside. Only the mute, spotlight lit the preserved body of Lenin in a clear-glass coffin.

"Sort of like a butter dish," Fenton remarked.

"It is kinda eerie in this light," Billy said nervously.

"Yeah, and get a load of this Lenin guy's wormy face!" added Rossiter. "No wonder nobody comes to look at him anymore!"

Sturgis walked closer to the bier and saw clearly that Lenin was covered with a virulent green mold. He was half-eaten away by rats or bugs, too.

"Kinda sad, ain't it," Fenton offered. "Not like the tourist brochures I've seen."

"Aw, he never was no Snow White anyway," Billy spat.

Fireheels reached through a cracked area of the glass and touched the body's left arm. It disintegrated, sending out a cloud of gray dust.

"Phew! Cut that out, Fireheels," Billy said.

"Okay, enough!" Sturgis snapped. "Come on and gather around me. Now the first thing to do is for two of us—you're the right sizes Martino and Farris—to get in the dead goose-steppers' uniforms. Go out there and start parading around. I'll send two guys to spell you in an hour."

The two troopers selected frowned, but knew it had to be done. Everything at the tomb must appear normal.

Tranh and Henderson had remained with the

trucks, fully protected by their C.A.D.S. suits. Any trouble and they would fire a shot.

He had, Sturgis felt, pulled the quick operation off without any Sovs seeing a thing! So far, so good! Now to look for the alleged tunnels.

When the ersatz guards left, Sturgis said, "Okay men, the plan is this . . ."

CHAPTER 23

Rossiter, the most curious by nature of all the troopers, started poking around. He went through the office of the slain tomb guards and briefly inventoried their possessions.

"Hey, Skip, these guards had all the comforts of home. This place is full of food, candy bars, too, and they have the local newspaper." His words echoed like a Swiss yodeler.

"Keep looking around," Sturgis said. "Maybe there's something we can use."

While the other men and Sturgis were loading their C.A.D.S. suits' firing systems with the Soviet ammo from the stores, and then searching for the alleged ancient tunnel into the Kremlin, Zandark began studying the old map he had brought. After studying the half-crumbling diagram showing the tunnel in relation to the tomb, the old Uzbec leader took up his massive wooden staff. He hit the marble floor in a dozen places, until it sounded hollow.

"Dig here!" he proclaimed. "Is tunnel!"

Henderson and Kendricks used their alloy-steel fingers to smash in the flooring and pry out bits of stone. After a few feet, they hit a hollow.

"I think we found the tunnel!" Henderson exclaimed. He and Kendricks put on their helmet strobes and peeped in. "Sure looks like an old brickwork tunnel, colonel," Henderson added.

"Good work. All of you!" Sturgis replied, coming over.

Mickey Rossiter, who had continued to delve into the files and cabinets in the guards' office, found nothing of use. So he sat down at the desk, put his feet up and slowly perused the pages of *Pravda*. On page four, he found something startling.

"Hey Skip!" he shouted, "I found something you're not gonna believe! It's a picture of a woman. It looks like—well, isn't this *Robin,* your wife?"

Sturgis, who had just disassembled his konked-out helmet strobe to fix it, put it down on the mausoleum's edge and strode into the office. "Let me see that, Mickey," he exclaimed, as he took the newspaper. The picture in it was of a dark, beautiful woman in handcuffs. A badly exposed black and white picture, but it *was* Robin! He was sure of it. What was she doing in *Pravda?*

"What's it say, Wosyck? My Cyrillic is worse than my spoken Russian." The Pole had come in shortly after the colonel.

"Hmm . . . says this American woman was arrested in the Arkansas district of occupied U.S.A. for burning a Russian flag. Let's see . . . it goes on to

160

say that the new soviet premier, Sergei Menshekov, ordered the arrest of this 'defiant' woman as an example to others who resist liberation. She is in Moscow, it says, to be interrogated in the Kremlin's special political detection area! It's today's paper, Skip!"

"Robin is *here* in the Kremlin!" Sturgis gasped. "There's no doubt about it. She was in Arkansas last I heard, but the picture is definitely her!" The commando colonel nearly fell backward with the realization. "This changes everything! We can't blow up the Kremlin until I go in and get her out of there!"

"Don't do it, Skip!" Rossiter objected. "You'd never find her."

Sturgis grimaced and said slowly, "I'm *doing* it. I'm in command, Mickey. I'm going in alone, without a C.A.D.S. suit, disguised as a Soviet. I'll make it quick—only check the cell areas—"

"But Skip," Mickey began.

"No buts! If I'm not back in an hour and a half, Tranh comes in and wrecks the place, as we planned. Total destruction of all the targeted buildings. Especially the premier's office."

Zandark strode in and asked something Sturgis couldn't catch. Wosyck translated. "He said, 'Why you not take super-suit?' I guess he heard what's up, Skip; sound travels here."

"I want to keep our presence here a surprise. If they seize me, well it's just one man. They'll think I'm just a spy. Besides, a suit won't help me find Robin. I will use the tunnel, pop up and bop a Russkie on the head, use his clothes. I have to try! She's my *wife,*

161

Goddamm it!"

The Uzbec headman said, "I go in with you." He rattled off a long statement, gesticulating wildly.

"He said," Wosyck translated, "that his grandfather was arrested in the 1991 purge and was imprisoned here. Last word about him was in 1996. They said he was still alive. Zandark wants to look for him. He says it is his blood, so he goes, too."

Sturgis nodded. "Okay, Zandark. Come on in with me, you Uzbec maniac! We'll make a good team!"

Fate, the colonel realized, had given him this one more chance to reclaim Robin. He would *not* fail!

The troopers who had been digging pushed aside the gathered stones, and the tunnel was revealed more clearly. Sturgis shined the strobe down into a damp-looking brick passage and exclaimed, "God, the tunnel is still in decent shape! We can make it."

Sturgis and the Uzbec descended into the pit and, as Tranh said a quick, "good luck," they moved off down the snaking mold-lined passageway. The way was cramped, foul-smelling and dank as a sewer.

After a hundred yards, it grew so narrow that Sturgis was about to order a return to the tomb. Then he saw a crack of light. It was the edge of a rusty old door that must have been designed for midgets.

"Well, this is it, Zandark," Sturgis said, spitting on his hands for luck. "We will see where we come out. Either we will have a reception committee, or we'll be in luck. Here goes!" He pushed open the small door. It fell off its hinges and down onto a dusty floor. They were in a dim—what?

"Looks like a kitchen pantry, Zandark."

The Uzbec nodded, though Sturgis supposed he hardly understood, except by inference, what the colonel said. They stealthily crossed the dim-lit room; and Sturgis turned a doorknob. He opened a wooden door onto a long electric-bulb-lit corridor. They kept their pistols ready as they went rushing down the hall to a single oaken door made of heavy beams.

"I think this is the entrance," Sturgis said, "to the dungeon. Let me look at that map again." Sturgis, using his flashlight, consulted the map and, reassured, nodded. "So far so good! I know where we are."

The heavy door creaked open when Sturgis and Zandark both put their weight against it, and they found themselves at the top of a winding set of descending bluestone stairs. The colonel saw a flickering orange light below. He motioned to Zandark with his index finger over his lips. Zandark nodded. They tried to make no noise descending, holding their guns at the ready.

They needn't have bothered being stealthy. Sturgis realized that when he saw the contents of the foul-smelling torchlit chamber: just one shackled skeleton and a lot of hungry rats that scattered as they came to the floor.

Sturgis examined the skeleton chained to the wall. The victim had been dead a year at least. He noted that the skeleton had a ring on one of its fingers. It was not gold or silver; just made of beaten steel. That was probably why the Sovs didn't take it.

Zandark let out a gasp and pointed to the ring, then to his own index finger. Zandark wore an exact copy of the skeleton's ring! "You know this—man? Sturgis asked.

"Grandfather!" Zandark whispered in a trembling voice. He took the ring from the skeleton and kissed the skull. "Peace, peace," he mumbled. Then he put the skeleton's ring on his other hand. "Is good to know." There was moisture in the corner of the Uzbec's brown eyes.

Sturgis pulled him onward. Zandark had found *his* relative; now it was Sturgis's turn. He had to find Robin.

There was a corridor of rough-hewn stones to the left—and they found another cell door at the end of it.

Sturgis found a set of well-worn keys hanging on a steel peg in the wall. The third key fit the cell. Inside the cell was a sight that made Sturgis wretch. There was a bloated, naked corpse, chained to the wall. The bald man's torn and rent purplish skin crawled with roaches. He had electric wires leading from a hand-driven generator in a corner attached to its rotting testicles. The colonel hit the Off switch. A week too late for this guy, Sturgis thought. He noted some other grim clues to the torture the bug-eyed corpse had endured: There was a plastic cup of water just out of reach of his hands, rigged on a pulley, so that every time he leaned forward to take a drink, the water moved away. That and the genital electric shocks must have driven him stark raving mad. What did they do this to him for? Burning a flag?

Not saluting?

They tried more cells and found more bodies. One prisoner had his guts pulled half out of his stomach and wrapped around a motor-driven wheel, the controls of which were set for an inch an hour of slow pull. He had been alive just recently—no smell.

The intruders had seen all there was to see of this area and ascended to the first corridor once more. They continued on, until they found a new red-painted door marked in Russian, Foreigners. One of the keys Sturgis had brought up from the torture den below fit in the lock. They entered the cell and received a start. A man—alive this time—jumped up. He cringed in fear, backed off, saying, "No! No more!" in English.

The man had a khaki uniform with U.S. Air Force markings on it.

"Who are you?" Sturgis asked.

"You speak English without an accent?" The uniformed man's shoulders went down a bit from their protective posture. "I'm—I'm Neil Ryan, an American flyer." He composed himself a bit and continued: "Who the hell are you? And who's your beefy pal?"

"Dean Sturgis, commander of the U.S. C.A.D.S. commando unit. We're here to kill the premier and to destroy the Kremlin. This is—an ally of ours. We're searching for prisoners first. You're our first find, Ryan. Congratulations. Do you know of any others still alive? A woman?"

"You don't know how welcome you are! I've been here since my plane got shot down when we counterattacked Russia! It's been hell!" Sturgis now saw how gaunt the man was, how sunken his eyes.

"Any others alive?" Sturgis insisted.

"No—no. They all—wait! A woman was brought in last week. They took her right past here—heading to the right. There's special cells down there. I know because I heard her speak English." Ryan sat back down on his mattressless, iron-mesh bed frame, breathing hard.

"How come there's no guards around?" Sturgis asked.

"They hate the damp; they leave for days, leaving us without food or water."

"Okay buddy," Sturgis said. "Can you walk? Here, try some of this." Sturgis gave him some of the wolf meat broth from his canteen.

Ryan gulped it until it was pried away.

"It tastes great! What is it? Mutton soup?" asked the pilot.

"Something like that, Neil. It's full of vitamins. But go easy." The colonel handed the canteen back.

Soon, Sturgis had the American flyer walking. The colonel knew that Ryan wasn't fit enough to come along in the search. What could he do with the pilot? In a moment, he decided. The only course of action was to give Ryan the map. "That tunnel," he pointed out, "will take you to my men. Good luck."

"Good luck to you guys, too. And watch out for Glassnose!"

"Who's Glassnose?" Sturgis asked.

"The worst of the torturers," the pilot replied. "Some of the guards aren't that bad, for Russkies. But he's a sadist. Shoot him *first*. You didn't—didn't hear the pleas—the screams!"

166

"How do I tell who he is?"

Ryan smiled. "That's easy. Glassnose has a clear plastic nose—a replacement of his real schnozola after some sort of plane crash. He was a interceptor pilot in the war. He hates Americans more than anything in the world. I suppose one of us shot him down!"

"Don't worry, Ryan, I'll shoot him first! Thanks pal."

As the pilot limped off toward the tunnel, Sturgis and Zandark went toward where the woman prisoner had been taken.

CHAPTER 24

As Sturgis and Zandark moved onward, they thought they were unseen. But eyes watched through a hole in the stone walls, twin blue beacons of hate. And between those eyes of evil was a long, clear plastic nose, revealing pulsing veins and fluids.

Glassnose motioned with his hands to his two assistants, Medrev and Sunin. Medrev, the youngest of the black-clad officers of the elite Kremlin Guard, moved away silently along the secret passageway to follow alongside Ryan. Sunin and Glassnose tagged along parallel with the two tall intruders who had freed the pilot. Glassnose was intrigued, and pleased to have these two new—*subjects*.

The torturer rushed along until he and his comrade exited ahead of the intruders into the corridor. Then he and Sunin raised their huge three-inch barreled weapons and fired.

Sturgis and the Uzbec chief heard a pop and saw a

shell skitter from the distant recesses of the hallway and hit the floor beneath their feet. White choking smoke poured out of it when it burst open.

"Gas!" the colonel yelled. "Let's . . ."

Then he couldn't speak or breathe, and he blacked out—before he hit the stone floor.

Sturgis woke up chained hand and foot to a wall. He shook his head repeatedly to clear his vision, and when he could see, he saw Zandark was chained next to him. He was now coming around, too. Sturgis started to focus on a hulking shape when a crushing hand slammed his head back against the wall.

A raspy voice snarled, "Ah, coming around are you? Heh! Now we find out who we grabbed. They are two strange types, don't you think so, Alexi?"

"Yes, Glassnose. Strange," agreed the coldly handsome Alexi Sunin. Sturgis felt the crushing hand let go of his face and he beheld the countenance of a round-faced hirsute middle-aged man. He wore a black uniform covered with skull and crossbone medals and ribbons. The jowled cheeks were pockmarked with acne-craters; the eyes were blue headlights of evil, the outward manifestation of a mentally deranged brain behind it. And the man had a clear plastic nose, dripping with mucus.

"So you are Glassnose," Sturgis said. "I like your purple-dyed mohawk haircut. But that went out of style in the eighties you know!"

"Ah—that is *good*. You are a spunky American, aren't you? Perhaps you are another flyer—heh? Or a spy trying to rescue your nation's M.I.A.s? You Americans are so dramatically sentimental, always

170

trying to rescue one another," Glassnose mocked, "And that is so stupid, for it only results in more of you being caught!" Glassnose turned to the bearskin coat-clad Uzbec. "And this other specimen of strangeness . . . where did you pick him up? In a circus?" Glassnose went over and lifted Zandark's head by the beard—and got spat on. He let go and wiped his sodden plastic nose with his hand. "You will pay for that, savage!" Zandark met his gaze with a fiery evil eye of his own.

Glassnose went over to a corner where a set of odd metal rods were heating over a fire. He lifted one, a pincer, and approached Zandark. A cruel smirk twisted his thin lips, but just then, a buzzer sounded. He hesitated, frowned.

"I have to go. Sunin, call some guards. Watch these men carefully!" Glassnose laughed. "You gentlemen will find the pilot you attempted to free with you soon! As for this cell, you will grow to love the place. It's a regular resort. Ha-ha! I will see you later!" He put the pincer back in the heater.

After he left, the captives were guarded by six burly Russians and the thin young officer. Sturgis immediately tried to get on the officer's nerves. He had noted that Sunin had responded to their English, so knew he would be able to understand.

"Hey *pervert*," Sturgis said, "do you sleep with Glassy nose? Are you his little toy?"

The officer pretended not to hear or understand. Sturgis kept at him. Zandark aimed a few saliva oysters at the soldiers with deadly accuracy and got himself kicked pretty bad. Sturgis too, repeatedly got punished with a fist to his gut for his insults. But

171

it was worth it, for Sturgis had been working one hand through the too-wide wrist shackles.

The third time the young Red's practiced fist hit his stomach, Sturgis pulled his hands free and the left one grabbed the man's throat in an iron grip. Years of practice, with the metal gloves deactivated on his C.A.D.S. suit to make them a grip-strengthener, now paid off. The man could barely breathe, and couldn't break free.

Sturgis's right hand seized the Tokarev pistol from Sunin's holster. "Now," Sturgis ordered, "release me or I'll kill this jerk-off!" With Sunin turning blue and nodding, the guards obeyed.

Glassnose, when he returned to find the cell open and the soldiers and Sunin dead, realized that the intruders had escaped. How, he couldn't imagine. But something had to be done about it. He summoned more troops to begin a search.

Several floors above him, another officer in a white laboratory smock stood over a softly sobbing auburn-haired woman tied to a strange, heavily wired metal chair. Robin Adler.

"I like uncooperative prisoners." He smiled. "It gives me a chance to learn new ways to inflict pain, to try out Glassnose's way of retraining her mind. Do you know, Miss Adler, why they call this the Ruby Laser Interrogation Room? It's simple! Because of the laser device here; a device that can reach into the various areas of a brain and make changes. That is why you are seated here, manacled head and foot, and ready to receive the brain-probe needles."

Robin braced herself as the smocked man said, "Try these little probes on for size. They will shoot laser light directly into your brain. You will feel pain, but it will not be so bad. But you will be unable to pass out. Don't resist. The pain goes on forever, until you . . . *change!"*

"No . . . please. Don't," she wimpered.

The technician busied himself clicking on circuits and adjusting dials on a panel, then returned to Robin.

Just as the lab man put on her headset and was adjusting it, the emergency phone rang. He picked up. "Yes?" he said. "What! At once, Glassnose." He put down the phone. He looked over at the wimpering American beauty in the torture seat.

"I am told we must postpone your training session. I must help search for some escapees . . ."

He left, not removing the unactivated mind-prober.

A reprieve, Robin thought. But only that. She would not be able to resist these devices. No one could. Slowly but inexorably, she would be made a tool of the Soviet will. A robot. Glassnose had already told her what her mission would be once she was an automaton: She would be sent to kill Dean Sturgis, her husband. And she would do it!

While Glassnose's floor by floor search of the Kremlin mazes proceeded, Zandark and the colonel were making their way toward Robin. The half-dozen soldiers they surprised in the Q corridor were cut down gunfighter style with commandeered Tokarev pistols. Each of the Freedom Fighters had a

173

hot gun in both hands and fired mercilessly. Soon they were less than fifty feet from Robin's cell, desperately continuing their search for her. Ryan had given only vague directions.

Zandark ran smack into the lab man who had just left Robin waiting under the brain-altering machine. The smocked torturer didn't even get a chance to shout; his larynx was crushed by the giant Uzbec's eager massive hands. Then Sturgis found the lab room with its door unlocked.

They strode in, ready for anything. And Sturgis saw the torture chair and the woman strapped into it, her head half concealed by a cold, steel helmetlike device full of blinking lights and wires. He carefully lifted the mechanism.

"Robin!" he gasped. He tore off her bindings, smashed the headgear from her head onto the concrete floor of the lab.

"Is it really you, Dean?"

He crushed her to him. "Yes, Robin. It's me! *Really.*"

"But how?" Her amber eyes widened to take him in.

"A long story, Robin."

"I—I love you, Dean. Oh God I do! That other time when, when I said I didn't—I realize now that I was being manipulated, drugged. When it wore off, I thought only of you, Dean! They used psychological methods on me, to make me not care for you."

"Then Danirov isn't your—you aren't in love with Danirov?"*

"No; it's only you, Dean. Oh, how I love you!
* See C.A.D.S. #5.

Never let me go!" Her tears flowed freely now; sweet rivers of relief.

"I won't, Robin. I won't. Fate has given me this chance to be with you and I'll never leave you. Come on. Can you walk?"

"I don't think so."

"I'll carry you then." He swept her up in his arms and headed out the cell door. She felt weightless.

With Zandark taking the point, they rushed through the hallways of the dank underside of the Kremlin, back toward the secret tunnel leading to the tomb—and safety.

Sturgis was worried. He didn't know what time it was. They had taken his watch. But he was sure it was way past the time that he had to get back to the tomb. The whole place would be attacked and blown up any minute by the C.A.D.S. force.

And himself and Zandark and Robin along with it.

CHAPTER 25

But the grim reaper stayed his bloody scythe. For they ran into Billy and his team of five men near the tunnel. They were pulling along an extra suit. Sturgis quickly started to explain the situation. Billy said, "I know the score, Skip. Lieutenant Ryan made it to the tomb. Glad to see you got to Robin!"

Sturgis thought a second, then said, "Right!" He turned to Zandark. "Put up your hands, chief," he said. He shoved Robin into the big brute's hold and gave her a quick kiss. "You're going back with him— we have a staging base outside the Kremlin. I've got business here with the Soviet's head butcher!"

"I don't want to leave you," Robin pleaded. "Never!"

"Has to be. Trust me. I'll be back." He started to outfit himself with the C.A.D.S. suit as he spoke.

As the Uzbec carried Robin off to safety, Sturgis said, "Okay men, let's fuck up this place."

"Where to, Skip?" said the eager Southerner as Sturgis snapped his helmet into place. The colonel

177

replied, "First, we have to go upstairs and pay some surprise visits to the other officials who started World War Three. We'll go to their offices. The layout of the Kremlin is programmed into your C.A.D.S. computers. I hope they haven't altered it too much since the C.I.A. got that data a few years ago."

"Now you're talking," Rossiter said.

The C.A.D.S. men left the subterranean passage via five swirling flights of stairs and stepped out into the pale sunlight of a winter's day. They were on the street level, near a Gothic building. Smack dab in the middle of the Kremlin.

"So we hit this building?" Fireheels asked.

"No. Check the plan, Fireheels! That's for team two, when they come through five minutes after us. We go to the Presidium; the other end of the Kremlin!"

Sturgis had his five elite fighters make a beeline for the designated free-fire zone marked Area A on the computer generated three-dimensional map projected on his visor screen.

Now Soviet soldiers on routine patrol became aware of their presence and started small-arms fire from several positions. The bullets just bounced off the C.A.D.S. warriors' black steel armor, and their weapons systems clicked on, tracked the enemy, and returned SMG fire with deadly accuracy without the Americans breaking their stride. The war had been brought home to its instigators.

Sturgis had reserved this plum of the poison tree, the Presidium Building, for his A team. Hopefully they'd catch the premier himself in his office there.

Power-driven steel boots raced along the hallowed grounds of Empire, and soon they stood before the sleek modern white marble and black glass structure. Alerted by the earlier gunfire, soldiers were pouring out of its main doors, firing every conceivable sort of weapon. Sturgis smiled as he targeted an E-ball for the closely packed group of Sov killers. He felt the reassuring *chunk* of the fifteen pound explosive charge fitting itself into the weapons-tube attached under his right arm. He lined up the sight in his visor and commanded, "Fire E-ball!"

The hellfire of the electrically charged "hot" shell blew all the fifteen gathered Sovs into pieces of burning flesh and bones and melted rifle parts. Plus it blew out a fifteen-foot circular hole in the building wall! Glass fragments were still cascading down when they moved on.

"Forward, men," Sturgis said softly. "I've got another E-ball for Premier Belyakov!"

The six C.A.D.S. warriors strode across the flowerbeds, crushing the red and white geraniums which were a puzzlement until Sturgis realized they were heated by warm air from below. Sturgis noted the floral display was in the shape of a red hammer and sickle. They were about to step through the gaping hole in the Presidium Bilding's wall when there was a roar. No—more like a grinding.

"Blue-mode," the colonel said, knowing darn well what it was.

The blue-mode indicated that coming up behind the Presidium were two huge slow-moving metal shapes, followed by a hundred blue triangles.

"Computer, identify," he asked.

Troops with bazooka, and several heavy armored vehicles.

"Identify heavy vehicles with GI-mode," Sturgis ordered.

T-45 tanks, the computer replied. *What else?*

"Hold it men. Let 'em get to us, so we can line up our E-ball sights!"

The first T-45 rounded the corner and the raspy voice of Glassnose called out over one tank's PA system, "Give up, intruders, and we will not kill you." Sturgis saw a blue sprig of hair jutting from the trapdoor of the first tank.

Sturgis smiled. "E-ball those tanks, Billy."

"With pleasure," smiled the South's favorite son from behind his tinted visor. He whispered the commands to his computer and released a cometlike messenger of death across the courtyard separating the C.A.D.S. force from their assailants. Glassnose had been observing the strike force from atop his tank when the lightning flash filled the lenses of his binoculars. He barely had time to gasp. His crystalline proboscis reflected a prismatic glint from the approaching electro-shell in the millisecond before impact. Then, Glassnose was canceled, as the tanks and their crews, vaporized in a stew of steel and guts.

Billy raised his weapons-tube to his helmet and gave a cavalier whiff, like a gunfighter blowing smoke from his six-shooter.

"Good shooting, white man," said Fireheels, who had viewed the destruction from a perch on a large, decorative planter nearby.

"Thanks chief," replied Billy.

"Save the kudos for the debriefing," Sturgis ordered over the com, "and load your Variable Shell-Firing systems with those tanks ammo. This place is gonna get hotter than a Tijuana whorehouse from here on in." Following the lead of Sturgis, the A team members, Billy, Rossiter, Fireheels, Martino, and Berk, plundered the spilled shells of the T-45. It was good stuff—.105s and 44mm. explosive rounds. Once done they looked to their screens. The medieval citadel was represented by a complex blueprintlike readout of the half-acre, triangular-shaped fortress of the czars. The honeycomb of walls, palaces, and courtyards, was awash in a sea of blue triangles and squares, indicating commie elements closing in on them from every direction.

Sturgis took in the whole field of operations with blue-sensor's eagle glance: Clouds of light artillery rushed forward in bewildering patterns; a column of armored vehicles streamed through the gates to support the tanks already in position; a dozen squads of elite Spetznaz soldiers were with them. The two other C.A.D.S. squadrons and the detachment of Uzbec irregulars were well into the fray. Sturgis realized he had a full-blown battle on his hands. Enough work for a division.

"Shootout at the OK corral, comin' up men," he stated. "Let's move."

Ignoring the threatening maneuvers of the powerful T-45s in the courtyard, Sturgis directed his troopers to follow as he led them from their exposed position into a nearby building.

"All right, men, listen and listen tight," said

Sturgis. "We're about to go in what's known as the Presidium. It's designated building three on your visor screens. You can see the other squads moving into position to plant their charges. Some of us go in, and others keep these boys occupied, savvy?"

Each squad member breathed his assent and routinely began opening channels to Sturgis's command computer so their leader could constantly monitor their status.

"Fireheels," said Sturgis, "you take Rossiter and Martino and move west along the wall toward the Borovitskaya Gate and intercept that column of armored vehicles moving in on us. Buy us as much time as you can, but if it gets too hot, retreat northward, staying inside the walls, if possible. Rendezvous with us at building fourteen; that's the ancient Oak Beam Hall, right across from where we are now. It's the oldest, most valued building in all of Russia, and chances are the Sovs will be hesitant using heavy fire on us if we hole up there. Remember, we're on sacred soil as far as the Russians are concerned. That's one thing we have on our side. They'll be looking to round us up with as little destruction as possible to their capitol. Keep moving, ride high in the saddle, and . . . have fun."

Sturgis watched as Fireheels and his team sped along a colonnade and disappeared into the maze of passageways, tunnels, and stairwells that interlinked the Kremlin palaces.

"Keep in touch," Sturgis reminded Fireheels over the com, then turned to Billy Dixon and the greenhorn Tommy-the Aussie-Berk. "Let's go guys," he said.

"Where?" asked Berk, mesmerized by the light show on his visor. "I feel like I'm in a video game."

"Into the eye of the storm," said Billy. "It's *real.*"

The three C.A.D.S. legionnaires bounded toward a wide marble staircase leading to the upper levels of the Presidium. By now the entire Soviet high command was alive to the fact that the unthinkable had happened: The inner sanctum of Soviet world power had been invaded by a gang of mechanized supermen!

Uniformed KGB agents supported by Moscow police and army regulars began streaming into the area. Already a dozen of the Spetznaz goons followed the fast-moving C.A.D.S. men up the stairs only to be doused in a wave of burning plastic from Tommy Berk's weapons-tube. The searing liquid fire clung to the pursuer's skin and clothing, and they tumbled screaming down the stairs as their flesh broiled "like shrimps on a barby." The confusion and panic these human torches caused in the foyer gave Sturgis and his men time to disappear, pushing aside robotic floor sweepers, who emerged from the hall's several rooms as the din of battle built, setting them in motion. A strange unexpected, funny sight.

Sirens blared now and police bullhorns called out warnings for civilians to clear the area, but the Muscovite civil servants and bureaucrats, incited by the disturbance to their endless tedium, poured out of offices and chamber rooms. Crowd control became a problem as the Soviet security forces, and they responded mindlessly to orders from their rigid command system. They simply mowed over throngs of people as they poured forth from the facades of buildings into the cramped alleys and courtyards at the north end of the Kremlin.

Half a dozen tanks, those remaining from Glassnose's detachment, had finally lumbered into position on a wide plaza that surrounded the Oak Beam Hall. The tanks surrounded the ancient structure, one of Russia's most revered national monuments. Sturgis realized that the tanks were assuming a defensive posture.

If Fireheels could block the main gate, the Russians wouldn't have more heavy equipment to counter their suits. He watched anxiously as his computer described Fireheels's progress indicating the Indian's path by a red line that winded slowly through the three-dimensional rendition of the Kremlin aglow on the C.A.D.S. suit visor.

"How goes it, 'heels?" he radioed.

The radio crackled and Sturgis could hear the rat-tat-tat of steel bullets dinging off the cadmium steel C.A.D.S. armor.

"Okeydoke this end, colonel," Fireheels responded. Then the *whoosh* of a liquid-plastic fire blast filled the airwaves. "Got some red-hot Reds on the lamb here. We're into some pretty narrow passageways now. At one point we could barely fit through with our suits on. It works to our advantage, though. Since we're impervious to their small-arms fire, we can take them on in the tight spots, one-on-one, and toss them aside like ducks in an oil slick. We're coming to a spiral staircase now. Resistance still spotty, but building."

"Do you copy that Sov convoy closing in?"

"Roger, Skip. I read sixteen big tanks, ditto troop transports, and one dozen even light cannon."

"Ahh . . . roger, Fireheels. Look . . . they'll be at division strength around here in minutes. Do you think you can waylay some of that parade?"

"We've cleared the stairway and looks like we got a clear run for a couple hundred yards or so," Fireheels replied. "We got a security guard down the far end of the hall taking potshots at us with a forty-five or something. Take him out, Rossiter . . ."

Sturgis cut the talk for a second to take out a Spetznaz commando training a bazooka at him, splattering his guts with chunks of human liver.

"Gotta go now, Skip," Fireheels said. "Got combat. Regular army. Computer: Relay to Sturgis our ETA at minimal effective deployment."

A printout appeared on the colonel's visor detailing Fireheels's situation: *Squad B will achieve effective deployment in three minutes, twenty-one seconds under present variables . . . Status fluctuating . . . Hostile transports will penetrate perimeter in two minutes, fifty-nine seconds. Estimate eight vehicles will face destruction.*

"Not bad," said Sturgis, "they should be able to cut off the brunt of their firepower. "Now, where those damn Uzbecs? I knew they'd be our weak link. They were supposed to rendezvous with us by now." The colonel, Billy Dixon, and Berk had reached their first objective, the roof of the Ambassadors Hall. Below them and just to the left on one side they overlooked the Oak Beam Hall and its cordon of Soviet tanks. Sturgis could see the mayhem that gripped the streets. There were no civilian auto-mobiles within the walls of the Kremlin, but the crunch of people, civilians, and soldiers, paralyzed the Soviet forces. The mission was off to a good start. They had effected complete surprise at the inner sanctum of the Russian Empire. Not since Napoleon had these walls been breached.

Sturgis turned and for the first time realized that he stood perched over two hundred feet above the Moskva River. It was choked with ice. He saw Moscow proper, outside the walls of the Kremlin. Obviously, the alarm had sped through the city. The colonel scanned police, military, and fire vehicles converging down avenues from every direction. As Sturgis stared at the enveloping chaos at their feet, he began to realize that they were on a suicide mission. So be it!

Sturgis glanced at his digital time readout. Another minute or two and he'd have to proceed without Zandark and his men. During planning, Sturgis had tried to persuade the Uzbecs to remain behind, since they weren't needed to scale the Kremlin walls. But Zandark was quick to point out that his men would be useful making room-to-room searches for the premier and other important Soviet leaders, and would also be able to scamper through the many passageways in the Kremlin walls too small for the C.A.D.S. warriors to travel through. Besides, Zandark claimed that the Uzbecs would attack with or without Sturgis's approval. Having traveled across Russia, they would not be denied glory.

Sturgis took the time to contact Fenton and

Tranh, who now were leading squadrons around the other side of the Kremlin, through the Granovitaya and Terem Palaces and into the Great West Hall. The C.A.D.S. plan was unchanged despite the awesome counterattack: Seal off the Kremlin, round up and kill as many Soviet leaders as possible, including the premier if he could be found, and then improvise an escape back through Lenin's tomb and out of the city. That seemed unrealistic now, but any plan is better than none. There could be enough of a panic so that the trucks could roll out of town unnoticed.

"Fenton . . . Tranh . . ." he signaled. "Report."

"Fenton here, colonel," said the Englishman. "Quite marvelous architecture here in the Terem Palace. Did you know that the wooden chandeliers in the ballroom here were actually turned on the lathe by Peter the Great himself?"

"Get him," said Berk. "A museum tour in the midst of the raid of the century."

"Report!" repeated Sturgis, businesslike.

"We're right on schedule," said Fenton. "Tranh is holding the upper floors of the Granovitaya Palace, but the lower levels are packed like cattle cars. Last I heard he was going toe-to-toe with a pack of KGB boys on the roof over there. My squad was able to jet-pack to the roof of the Terem. So far we've cleared the top two floors, finding mostly a bunch of petty bureaucrats as far as I can tell. No big fish yet. Outside it's like a May Day parade. They got wall-to-wall T-45's lined up like kewpie dolls in Coney Island. I count one, two, three brigades within eyesight from this window on the third floor.

The boys are taking a few pokes at them, but they're not firing back . . . yet. I think we've got them between a rock and a hard spot, colonel."

"Let's hope we don't get crushed," replied Sturgis. "Tranh? Everything coming up roses on your end, too?"

"Not quite, Skip," said Tranh against a background of shattering glass and belching fire. "We got a regular inferno raging just below us. And there's some army regulars holding us back with antitank weapons. If the premier was downstairs, he's escaped by now. I had no idea there'd be so many civilians around."

"Me neither," said Sturgis. "But from up here it looks like guards are starting to get the place cleared out a little. We have to act fast . . . eliminate the forces inside the walls and close the place off. My guess is they'll try to hustle off the head honchos with the mob. Tranh, did Zandark and his men get off on time?"

"We left them right on schedule. Gotta move, Dean. This place is on fire!"

Sturgis moved to where Billy and Tommy Berk were pouring volleys of fire into a stream of commie troops entering the building at ground level. It was too late for the Uzbecs to meet them now. They were cut off.

"Let's move," he ordered.

Zandark had left Robin in the safe hands of Amarr, Ryan, and several C.A.D.S. men at the Tomb, and entered the Kremlin. Now, nine eager

Uzbecs, led by Zandark, trudged through a dark narrow tunnel no more than four feet high. They were hopelessly lost in the bowels of the Kremlin, an underground city of torture chambers, sinister laboratories, and prison cells. The Uzbecs were hopelessly lost, but there was a purpose to their wanderings.

There was something that Zandark and the other Uzbec men knew, which they had neglected to tell Sturgis. Few Russians knew that the czar and his family were murdered in the very rooms the Uzbecs coursed through, or that many of the missing crown jewels of Russia had been hidden somewhere in the caverns and never rediscovered. Zandark, as tribal chief, could recite a full inventory of the priceless crown jewels. The Uzbec chiefs had taught their sons the list since the thirteenth century; Uzbekistan—where the jewels had been mined—naturally claimed them as their own!

Zandark knew he was in quest of six rubies, each the size of his fist, plus a dazzling assortment of emeralds, sapphires, and diamonds. Zandark was convinced he knew where the jewels were. His father had learned from an exiled member of the czar's household that the jewels had, indeed, been carried to the Kremlin cellars by the Princess Anastasia, who had them sewn into the hem of her heavy, floor-length skirt. The Uzbecs had made a pact among themselves to impound the sovereign cache if ever they had the chance.

Zandark carried a flashlight to illuminate the way through the dark, circular, stone tunnels. Occasionally they came to a fork or an intersection, and

Zandark would consult his map to make a decision. The thunder of combat and the wail of sirens from above gradually disappeared as the tribesmen penetrated deeper into the underground complex.

"Here," Zandark whispered in Russian to his cohort, pausing in the cramped quarters to indicate a spot on the map. "This is the meeting of five points the map illustrates. From here we can get definite bearings."

They scurried unmolested down the passage indicated on the map and came to a thick oak and iron door secured by a two-inch-thick locked bolt.

"Mucklu, come up here," Zandark hissed from his position before the barricade. The squat, muscular aborigine wearing red-stained leather wormed his way forward through his comrades to the door. Zandark merely shrugged his shoulder toward the portal and the man understood. He dug his short, thick fingers into crannies on the door and began pulling at it. Slowly, Mucklu's face reddened as he strained against the ungiving barrier. The veins in his hairy arms and trunklike neck bulged; sharp bursts sprang from his pursed lips.

For a moment, it appeared as if the powerhouse would fail, but then a telling creak in the hinges gave notice of the turning tide. Mucklu grunted, inhaled deeply, and let out a primeval scream. The surge of force broke the stalemate and the door popped free, sending the Russian strongman tumbling backward into Zandark and the others.

"Good work," said the Uzbec chief. "Now get off me!"

The tribesmen untangled themselves and crawled

190

into the opening. Zandark shined the light around the stone walls of the wide circular room. Nothing. It was completely empty.

"A curse on Lenin's beard," said one of the men. "We should have known. The treasure is long gone, looted by the Reds."

"No wait," said Zandark, walking along the walls, feeling around.

The men waited nervously, listening to distant rumbles and encroaching scurries as their leader probed the hewn circuit of the cavern. The room was a dead end at the terminus of the tunnel, and the Uzbecs were armed only with Kalashnikov rifles and army .45s. If the Reds cornered them, they were dead ducks.

"Hurry, friend," one of the men, watching at the doorway, called. "We are already late for our rendezvous with Sturgis, and I think the Reds are closing in on us."

"Quiet," hissed another. "Let the old man concentrate. Now is no time to lose our nerve. Our chances are slim in any case."

"Yes, but if we were with the Americans in their armored suits, we'd have a much better chance. What good are jewels to dead men?"

"Look!" cried someone in the darkness. All eyes turned to Zandark. The flashlight beam was trained on a spot where he clawed away with his knife, poking free loose mortar and stone.

A shot rang out, ricocheting off a rock in the room. The Uzbecs at the door returned fire, cutting down two Soviet soldiers advancing down the passage.

"Give up, you men," someone called from outside in Russian. "You are trapped. Come out now or we will gas you where you stand."

"He's bluffing," said an Uzbec.

They heard a *pop* down the way and a gray-metal soup can tumbled into the room, a sickly green gas issuing from it.

"Hurry Zandark!"

"Get rid of it!" the chief yelled, frantically poking at the wall.

Someone grabbed the cannister and whipped it back out the doorway into the tunnel. Gunfire and more cannisters followed. Russian soldiers poured into the sector, but the cramped passageways prevented them from mustering a decisive advantage over the Uzbecs. Some gas reached them and they started coughing. Two other men had joined Zandark at his task as the hole opened ever easier, the mortar giving way to loose fill. They tore eagerly at the sand and pebbles.

"It's here! I can smell it!" cried one man.

"Quiet and dig you fool!" gasped Zandark.

"Grenade!" someone screamed.

Ten pairs of eyes froze on the hissing metal pineapple as it tumbled into the room and came to rest squarely in the midst of the men. Their jaws locked as they looked death squarely in the face.

Mucklu took one for the team. The lovable troll-like juggler did the unthinkable, throwing his body on the bomb.

There was no time for remorse. Mucklu's guts splattered the ceiling but darkness cloaked the grim carnage. In a second, the men at the door were again pouring fire down the tunnel and Zandark was back at his digging.

For what seemed like an eternity, but was actually only another minute, the Uzbecs struggled under their impossible situation; the men at the door fending off the determined Russian advance in the gas-filled passage; Zandark and the others digging.

"Nothing! There's nothing in here!" one of the diggers screamed in a panic. "Let's get out of here!"

"Wait!" yelled Zandark, a certain excitement to his voice. "I've got something!"

He pulled forth a dusty metal box from the rubble. The Uzbecs cast quick glances as he wiped it clean. The container glinted in the light of the flash. It was gold, expertly tooled, and set with rich blue sapphires and burning red rubies. It was the size of a large cigar box, and Zandark felt by its heft that it contained a rich store. Slowly he pried it open. The men gasped. It was true. Six rubies rested in golden compartments, like eggs in a carton. Strewn about were gobs of baubles, some faceted, some smooth; solemn greens, serene blues, brilliant whites. Zandark snapped the box shut and slipped it into his belt.

"Let's go," said the simple, but resolute nobleman. "We are late for our meeting with General Sturgis."

The Uzbecs turned to confront their adversaries, a bevy of elite Kremlin guards gathered at the five-points junction. They had started to set up antitank guns to blow away the Uzbecs.

Directing a thick volley of fire down their path, the tribesmen began a desperate advance on the Russians. They hefted the big door up as a shield and began inching their way along, choking in the lingering gas. Their eyes ran with tears against the burning vapors and their throats contracted in spasms as they pushed forward, bullets splintering the door as they progressed.

Into the breach they struggled, bullets eating flesh wounds into the shoulders and thighs of the leaders. The automatic weapons spit mercilessly, shells powdering the walls. Zandark gritted his teeth and snarled.

"By Satan's tongue!" he roared, then led his men in an ear-piercing war cry. The cavern reverberated with their shrill, high-pitched wail. Their rough peasant fingers bent the triggers of their rifles; the barrels of their guns smoked and burned red hot. Spent cartridges covered the floor. The Uzbecs, expertly trained by Sturgis's men, emptied magazine after hot magazine, reloading in the dark confusion of battle with practiced hands. They concentrated waves of fire down the hall, managing to drive the palace guardsmen back into the five-points intersection.

The Uzbecs broke through. The fighting was hand-to-hand in the crowded junction. Streams of Soviet defenders pushed their way into the fray. There was no escape. The Uzbecs unsheathed their hunting knives and commenced to butcher their foes. Blood flowed in buckets as throat after throat tasted steel. Jugular veins popped, squirting warm red liquid into the eyes and beards of Zandark and his men. The chief held his knife in one hand and a .45 in the other. He cursed as he pushed through, crushing the Soviets back.

It was all teeth and nails as human carcasses piled high in the room. A wild panic seized the Russians. The Uzbecs possessed that spirit that carries the tide of battle. The same spirit that instilled the ancient Roman centurian Manilius, who alone defended the Tiber Bridge against an army of Etruscans. The same spirit that enabled a handful of Spartan hoplites hold the pass of Thermopylae against the Persian hordes of Cyrus. The same spirit that carried the men of Pickett's brigade past the Union lines at Gettysburg, for one brief moment of glory. Battles are not decided by numbers, but by courage.

Hysteria swelled the throats of the Soviet regulars. It spread like electricity through the several lengths of tunnel converging at the five points. The soldiers dropped their weapons and turned to flee. A frenzied melee ensued. Men grabbed and clawed their way to be first, kicking at those behind them. The men squirmed in the tunnels like maggots, the Uzbecs bringing up the rear in a carnival of slaughter. So thick were the bodies that the tribesmen had to take time to clear the dead in order to advance. *Still holding the door!*

Gradually, the way began to clear as the last Russians escaped to the surface.

"They'll regroup at the surface," Zandark said, taking time with his men to catch his breath in the fetid stench and heavy air of combat. They coughed and spat blood.

"Ay, they fight like weak women! What sort of men are these?" said one of Zandark's men.

"Huh," laughed the chief. "These men are god-less. Their loyalty is to themselves. We need not fear them."

"Let's go!" the men shouted in unison. "Advance!"

They pushed forward into the basement of the Golden Hall, a large palace facing Red Square behind a cavalcade of terraces and stairways. Zandark rushed out firing his Kalashnikov but to his surprise, the room was empty. The Russians wanted no more of the mad Uzbecs.

A staircase led to the main floor, where Zandark gazed through a window at Red Square and got his bearings. Sturgis had pointed out the building where they were supposed to rendezvous: the Ambassadors Hall. The Uzbec chief identified the building, sitting kittycorner to the south, and he scanned the roof for signs of the C.A.D.S. leader. Nothing.

"They must have pushed on without us," said Zandark, spotting Russian soldiers at the windows on all floors of the building.

"Let's get to the roof," said Zandark. "Maybe we can spot General Sturgis from up there. Fun, isn't this?"

"Da!" agreed his smiling band of warriors.

CHAPTER 26

"You don't know how good it feels," said Billy, pumping a dose of teflon-coated 9mm lead at a quartet of Russian infantrymen, "to be taking on the beast himself right in his lair." Sturgis, too, felt the elation of long-held-back vengeance. His hot weapons-tube dealt fierce swathes of vengeance on his own targets. The C.A.D.S. squad, led by Sturgis, had left the roof of the Ambassadors Hall through a hidden staircase they found by chance in a medieval stone parapet anchored at the northeast corner of the building and opening toward the center of the Kremlin. With Billy at the point and Tommy Berk to the rear, the kill-knights ducked their way down a series of stairs, tossing guards over the stairwells or smashing skulls against the stone walls with blows from their powerful alloy arms.

As they exited the tower onto a narrow roadway leading to the main square of the Kremlin, Sturgis could see the Oak Beam Hall to his left and beyond that the Borovitskaya Gates, where a column of tanks were beginning to enter, crushing through a thick crowd of people attempting to flee. Berk leveled his right arm and dispersed a sizzling E-ball on a track not four feet above the cobblestone plaza. The electro-charged hunk burned a path of death through the throngs and caught the tank dead-square to rights in the nose. The electrified bucket of bolts exploded as its fuel and ammo stores ignited. The smoke, however, cleared to reveal three new Soviet tanks coming abreast, crushing screaming people under treads. Sturgis, Billy, and Tommy each delivered .105 shells, then turned without looking to see them explode.

"That should stuff up the gate long enough for Fireheels to get into position," said Sturgis. "Let's hit the Presidium. We should be able to corner some high-level rats there. Maybe even the Big Daddy."

The crowd in the alleyway separated in stunned fear as the C.A.D.S. men stormed through the twisting narrow street to the Presidium. Sharp-shooters and guards took shots at the Americans as they made their way. These Russians lacked the firepower necessary to take out the heavily armored C.A.D.S. suits. But there was a ring of T-45s anchored around the Oak Beam Hall. For a moment, Sturgis and his men were within the range of one of the tanks, and it turned its turret to zero in on them. But when the C.A.D.S. men moved on, the tank failed to fire. From windows and rooftops, Red officers and police shouted into their radios. "We need help! The Americans rule the battle! Send bazookas! Antitank weapons! Helicopters! We need heavy artillery! These invaders are like walking battleships!"

By now, Fireheels was securely in position, and he, along with Tranh's squad facing Red Square on the opposite side of the Kremlin, were keeping outside forces at bay.

Sturgis and his men bounded up the wide steps leading to the doric colonnade fronting the classic acropolis. Without hesitating, Billy lowered a shoulder and bulled through the towering wood and iron doors. The three men found themselves in a vast lobby lit by towering windows and encircled by a balcony along the second floor. Standing shoulder to shoulder along the full perimeter of the balcony stood some two thousand troops, the flower of the Kremlin's Spetznaz Guard, like the Green Berets their nation's most elite fighting force.

Instantly, a shower of gunfire rained down on the C.A.D.S. men. The sheer rapidity and volume of fire caused the men to jerk clumsily in their suits. The commies spewed venom by the pound, threatening to, if nothing else, bury the intruders under a curtain of spent shells. The Americans struggled to recover, tumbling backward out the door, regrouping, raising their weapon-tubes, and doggedly reentering, directing their own murderous spray at the Russians.

The Reds cowered beneath the stone facing of the balcony as SMGs bit chunks of stone away. The C.A.D.S. force advanced in workmanlike fashion. Finding a stair leading to the balcony, the armor-suited men ascended. The Russians offered a token resistance at first, but when Billy and Berk started one way around the balcony, and Sturgis went the other, delivering their SMG blasts, the Russkies went A.W.O.L. The C.A.D.S. men mowed them down mercilessly as they fled, or dove over the ballustrade, thirty feet down to the stone floor below.

"Don't waste ammo," Sturgis breathed. "Their crossfire causes their own destruction."

Sturgis and his men patiently eliminated the Praetorian Guard to a man before proceeding to the Central Chambers on the third floor. Sure enough, when the colonel kicked his way in, a full session of party bureaucrats huddled in the auditorium's velvet seats. One imperious-looking party chief made a pretense at authority.

"How dare you burst into this hallowed chamber of law, this palace of the workingman, this sacred altar of the people . . ."

Sturgis raised his left arm and fired a single six-inch steel dart, which pierced the man's thorax and came to rest in a wooden post behind him. The speaker fell face first, dead on the table.

"You sure got a way of taking charge at a meetin', Skip," muttered Billy.

"Who are you!" cried one of the Presidium members.

"What do you want from *us?*" screamed another.

"We capitulate!" hollered a third.

Sturgis switched to ampli-mode and silenced the crowd with his deafening declaration. "You men are guilty of crimes against humanity," he intoned. "Execute them, Billy."

"But we had nothing to do with the war!" cried the commie backbenchers. "We could not stop the Premier!"

"And where is the premier?" asked Sturgis, feigning the possibility of mercy for the treacherous.

"In his private office! The czar's study at the Oak Beam Hall!" the Presidium answered in unison.

"Interesting, and convenient," said Sturgis. "Execute them, Billy."

"But why?" a desperate comrade pleaded.

"When you accepted the mantle of office," declared the colonel, "you accepted responsibility for the actions of your government, like it or not. Your government, unprovoked, purposely and barbarously destroyed a nation of two hundred and sixty million miserable lives."

Billy ordered up liquid plastic fire from the computer's death menu and trained his left arm on the sniveling mob.

"Fire . . ." he ordered.

The Americans felt no remorse as the crematorium-fire erupted. Sturgis's mind flashed back to the dismal expanse that was now their homeland, the once beautiful America. The world's most fruitful farmlands now endless deserts; the towering cities charred graveyards to millions of souls; the proud people reduced to crazed mutant tribes wandering aimlessly across the poisoned landscape. If the Russians chose to destroy civilization, they must now taste the vengeance of the creatures of doom they created. Sturgis and Berk joined in the execution, each training their LPF streams onto the shrieking mound of frenzied creatures. Several broke free and ran among the tiered chamber in flames, the gooey liquid dripping from their flesh.

When the deed was done the three C.A.D.S. men shut down their flames and stood solemnly as the last death throes of arms and legs twitched in the human embers.

Sturgis accessed blue-mode. The flow of Soviet vehicles into the Kremlin had been cut off. He could read Fireheels's squad moving on the armored vehicles within the walls. That meant the Indian felt the Borovitskaya Gates were effectively sealed off for the duration of the mission. Tranh had managed to keep the Soviet forces massed on Red Square at bay while Fenton had nearly completed his movement along the West Wall. In a half hour, the crack C.A.D.S. force had thrown a cordon of chaos around the Kremlin, sealing the Red capital off with them in control.

"Skip!" cried Billy. "Look! It's the Uzbecs!"

Sturgis strode to the window and looked out onto the roof of the building across the way. Sure enough, the Uzbecs were gathered on the roof of the Golden Hall, trying to hold off a platoon of Reds in the square below who were moving on the building entrance. Sturgis trained his SMG on the enemy squadron and let loose a hale of fire, mincing them where they stood.

"Zandark," Sturgis called on ampli-mode. The chief looked up and spotted the C.A.D.S. leader.

"Zandark!" Sturgis repeated, summoning his best Russian. "Lead your men downstairs, then back across that courtyard into this building. We'll cover your crossing, then meet you on the main floor. Is Robin safe?"

Sturgis could see the Uzbec leader shake his head *yes* and move out.

"I hope the hell he understood," said Sturgis. "Cover him. Clear that square of hostiles . . ."

The three C.A.D.S. men went to work at the windows, picking off anything that moved on the plaza separating the two buildings. In a minute, the Uzbecs emerged from across the way.

"Skip!" laughed Billy. "They're walking backward! Why?"

"I don't know," replied Sturgis, gaping at the tribesmen as they tramped in unison across the courtyard. "I guess they got my Russian wrong," Sturgis laughed.

The Uzbecs crossed in safety and Sturgis met them as planned.

"What happened to you bums before? You were supposed to meet us at the Presidium."

"We got . . . lost . . ." mumbled Zandark. "Kill many commie though! And Robin, she safe, good protect. I leave good men!"

Sturgis noted the tinge of hurt in Zandark's tone. "Well . . . stick by us here on in. Where's Mucklu?"

"Mucklu he die very brave," said Zandark. "Very heroic. Save all of us."

"I'm sorry he died," said Sturgis. "I lost some men, too."

"We go for premier now?" asked Zandark.

"Yes," replied Sturgis. "We go for premier now. Men, load up V.S.F.s with one-oh-fives and forty millimeter shells from those wrecked tanks!"

As Sturgis and Zandark led their men to the Oak

Beam Hall, the other C.A.D.S. teams kept the Soviets completely off balance as they rolled through building after building, wasting Reds, igniting fire, demolishing everything in sight. The Americans were on a rampage of vengeance. Priceless art was ripped from the walls; busts of commie leaders cascaded out windows onto the squares below. It was as if they could exorcize the place, take out their years of rage on the objects revered by the Evil Empire!

Fireheels and Greenwald worked their way to the peak of a medieval tower guarding the main entrance to the Kremlin. A circular staircase led them three hundred feet up to an attic, then out a window to a narrow catwalk circling the steep, leaded roof.

Without a pause, Fireheels crawled up the sleek sixty-degree incline and positioned himself alongside a brass statue of Ivan the Terrible at the peak of the tower, some 360 feet above the wild fracas on the Kremlin streets. He looked straight into the flank of a column of Soviet trucks and tanks, jammed along the narrow streets of Moscow leading to the Kremlin. Beginning with the trucks farthest back, Fireheels began lobbing E-balls at the Soviets.

"Open fire!" he called to Greenwald, who remained on the narrow walkway at the base of the roof. "Fire one-oh-fives!"

The young recruit turned on the tanks clustered closest to the gates and unloaded half the store of V.S.F. system shells on the first half-dozen tanks he saw. In a dazzling fireworks display, he released the high-explosive rounds in rapid succession, one-second intervals. Each slammed square into the topside of a tank turret. Once struck, the armor-clad behemoths seemed to speed up, out of control.

Then their fuel boiled and their artillery shells ignited, turning the tank into a huge bomb that breathed great circles of death. But more tanks approached the gate.

Fireheels signaled both Greenwald and Rossiter to zero in on the target he was feeding their computers. All three C.A.D.S. men concentrated a double load of E-balls at the base of the tall stone tower on the left side of the gates. The combined power tumbled the building, just as Fireheels had reckoned, piling tons of rubble atop the cluster of burning tanks and streams of people.

"That does it," said Fireheels over his radio to the C.A.D.S. troops throughout the city. "The Borovit-skaya Gates are closed." He waded through spent shell casings. "Let's head to our rendezvous with Sturgis."

Fireheels was about to slide down the roof when, to his horror, a shot from one of the T-45s outside the walls struck the catwalk just below gutsy Greenwald's footing. Until now, the Russians had avoided using heavy guns against this particular monument of the Kremlin. Apparently, they had changed their minds. The tempo of shells increased as Greenwald struggled to regain his balance. Fireheels saw he was about to go.

"Use your jet-pack," the Indian called, but the young man couldn't right himself. He went over the wall headfirst and his jet-pack misfired. He crashed to the ground at the base of the outside wall. He was a sitting duck. Fireheels slid to the walkway and peered over at his friend. He quickly began firing on the remaining Soviet tanks, but he was down to his last two E-balls, his only effective weapon against the Soviet supertanks. He took out two more tanks, but in seconds, half a dozen turrets had swirled into position and were about to blast him. Greenwald, in suicidal bravery, rocketed up to take the shells in front of Fireheels.

Greenwald was dashed to smithereens, his suit shattered, shorted wires flashing. The turrets ceased their roar, then whirred upright, taking aim on Fireheels. But Greenwald's death had bought time for the agile Indian. He dove inside just as the T-45s unleashed their payload. They blew a gaping hole in the tower masonry, but not before Fireheels escaped at a run down the staircase to where Rossiter waited.

"Where's Greenwald?" asked Mickey.

"Dead," replied Fireheels. "Paid me back for knocking me into the sea when we air-dropped."

"Let's move," suggested Rossiter. "We still have to clear those bogeys around the Oak Beam Hall before the colonel gets there."

The two professionals tabled their feelings over their lost comrade and proceeded with their mission. They worked their way quickly across the square and got in close to the ring of tanks. They had spent their arsenals of E-balls and had to take the tanks out some other way.

"Let's commandeer a tank," said Fireheels, motioning Rossiter forward as they rounded a corner to confront the behemoths.

They made a dash for one of the T-45s and

clamored onto it. Fireheels got his cadmium steel fingers under the hatch and pried it open, then grabbed the first Red he saw, the pilot, and pulled him up, crushed the man's skull with his iron grip. Blasts from his SMG canceled the other two crewmembers.

"We'll never fit in there," exclaimed Rossiter, peering through the narrow hatch into the tank compartment. "We'll have to de-suit."

"No way," said Fireheels. The two saw their *Probability of Destruct* readouts ignite as the two tanks flanking them spotted their attack and whirled their monstrous cannon around. The C.A.D.S. men dove for the ground as the barrels roared. The commies scored direct hits—on each other!

Mickey and Fireheels began to move on the other tanks when Austin's voice crackled over their radios.

"Stand clear . . ." said the excited sergeant. "We have you in view. We'll take out these tanks with E-balls."

In seconds the sharp words of high-tech destruction shouted good-bye to the last remnants of Soviet resistance within the walls of the capitol.

Sturgis and his team met with Fireheels and Rossiter outside the Oak Beam Hall in the heart of the Kremlin.

"Martino bought the farm . . ." said Rossiter. "It's a miracle I'm—"

"Amen," replied Sturgis.

"What now, Skip?" Billy said, wiping blood off his visor.

"Premier Belyakov's private apartment is in here, in the old czar's study. This way, gentlemen," he beckoned, heading into the ornate structure, stepping over sprawled bodies that had their wet, sticky innards splayed out for all to see.

Sturgis, firing a .105, smashed open the oak double doors embossed with gold hammer and sickles. And they stood face to face with a thick-looking seamless blast door! "This," said the colonel, "might take a little *doing!*"

Fenton's wing had fanned out along the West Hall. His five C.A.D.S. commandos then took to the long rooftop connecting the Terem Palace with the Hall of Lazarus. From there, it was only a jet-pack jump away to the Byzantine spires of an ancient cathedral overlooking the confluence of the Moskva River. An ice-clogged branch of that river separated the Kremlin from the entire western half of Moscow. It was the job of Fenton and his men to take out the three bridges that spanned the branch, cutting off Soviet reinforcements from that sector.

They jogged single file at the peak of the pitched rooftops, their steel feet doing massive damage to three hundred-year-old roof tiles. From their perch three hundred feet above the city streets, they held a panoramic view of west Moscow, the city sprawling out before them in a gently sweeping valley crowded with buildings, houses, monuments, and parks. The streets were congested with traffic of all descriptions, and people scurried about like ants on the cityscape at their feet, terrified by the fighting noises.

So steep was their position that the bridges at the foot of the walls were not visible to them.

"Hold on," Fenton ordered. "I'm going to take a look over the edge."

In an instant, the guardsman looped his winch line around the thick neck of a stone gargoyle and rapelled over the edge of the roof. Dangling in midair, he could spot two of the bridges, but the southernmost was hidden behind the towering cathedral that anchored the south and west walls of the Kremlin.

"We'll move down," Fenton replied as a tiny powerful mini-motor whirred him back upward. "I want to be in a position to hit all three bridges at once. Let's hurry. Truck convoys are closing in on us. Reinforcements."

In seconds, they reached the chasm separating them from the cathedral and jet-packed over, each landing on a different steeple. As they wrapped themselves into position, using their metal cables, the C.A.D.S. men gazed down the sheer stone walls at their feet. Below, an onion dome spread a dazzling field of mosaic tiles before them; and beyond that, like gift ribbons far below the Kremlin's wedding cake architecture, coursed the cold brown waters of the rivers.

"There . . ." said Fenton. "There . . . and there . . ." he said, targeting in each bridge on his men's computers. "Commence firing."

With icy precision the Americans fed a barrage of plastique-laden rockets and E-balls into the buttresses and trusses supporting the western bridges. Russian commanders in the city streets below gasped as they witnessed the violent onslaught. Their own city being pummeled before their very eyes! They scanned the Kremlin heights in disbelief, but as the bridges crumbled, the relentless C.A.D.S. men trained their fire on the city itself, inciting a panic throughout the entire sector of the city. The scent of panic was in the air, and the crack C.A.D.S. commandos used it to their best advantage. Their precision-timed raids at strategic points caused more terror, carnage in an ever-widening arc through the theater of operation. The Russian reserves were kept constantly off balance according to the plan, buying Sturgis time to search for Belyakov.

"West Wall secure," Fenton radioed routinely to the squad leaders. "Moving to secure point two."

The Kremlin forms a rough triangle in the heart of Moscow, with two sides flanked by waterways, the south by the Moskva River and the northwest by a branch of that river. Only the approach from the east, which embraced the broad expanse of Red Square, was directly accessible by land. In planning the attack, Sturgis knew that success demanded holding back reinforcements while the search for Belyakov proceeded.

Tranh van Noc, his second in command, had a good plan. The battle-seasoned Oriental had studied the situation and decided the key to the defense of the searchers lay in holding the Granovitaya Palace and the Treasury Building. After decimating token Russian resistance in the Golden Palace, Tranh had led his unit from that burning building as it collapsed, and positioned two of his men in the Treasury, while he joined his other two troopers in the Palace. While Sturgis, Fireheels, and Fenton began their rounds of destruction throughout the building, Tranh and his valiant men fought a running battle with a burgeoning army of Red troops that had thrown grapples and climbed from Red Square. At first, the Russians had not wanted to fire on the sacred walls. But as the battle raged, and building after building had become consumed by flames, the Russian brass realized the futility of delay. The Americans were gaining complete control of their capitol. Honor demanded retaliation! Oblivious to hitting their own troops, now, the Soviets drew heavy guns and tanks into echelons and began pummeling the thick granite and sandstone of the fortress with howitzers and cannon. They planned to blast an avenue into the citadel and run their hundred tanks up on that rubble causeway.

But Tranh had chosen his defensive line well. From his positions in the Palace and the Treasury, he commanded a sweeping view of Red Square and, firing confiscated shells from his V.S.F., was able to hold the Soviet ground forces at bay. He ordered his men to concentrate their fire along lines that dissected the square and prevented orderly maneuvering by the masses of troops and tanks crowding into the area from all quarters. They also picked off the climbers with SMG.

From windows and rooftops high above the square, the C.A.D.S. men rained down shell after shell, chopping up the landscape and freezing the

Russian troops in paroxysms of chaos.

Tranh could feel his weapon-tubes overheating as he pumped buckets of lead into scrambling throngs of soldiers. The gutters ran with blood and bodies piled in mounds as the flower of Russian manhood met its end in Red Square that day.

A row of sixteen pale blue blips on Tranh's visor indicated the awesome slaughter was going to be intensified.

"Save your fire," he ordered his men. "Bogeys at three o'clock."

Soon, tele-mode told the fearful story. The blips were revealed as the Sovs' latest type aircraft. The first wing of Sov choppers broke over the eastern horizon, just skating rooftops with their death-laden steel bellies. Sixteen AR-56 Firespitter-attack helicopters were on their way in, four waves of four abreast. Tranh asked his computer for an inventory of his squad's antiaircraft arsenal.

At present, troops can access fourteen independently targeted ground-to-air missiles capable of eliminating intruders . . . the computer responded. It rattled off the names of the C.A.D.S. men carrying the AA-missiles.

"Good," said Tranh, who expected his men to have even less missiles left. "Make 'em count, boys. Stay plugged in to each other's targeting systems to avoid doubling up on the same ship. Let's hit 'em quick. Maybe we can scare a couple off . . ."

The Americans opened fire as the first wing of choppers cleared the row of ancient slabstone houses fronting the square. Four mini-stinger missiles issued forth from the Kremlin walls, streaking thin vapor trails. They met their separate prey in unison, eradicating the Soviet Firespitters before they could get off a shot. The doomed quartet exploded in midair and plummeted to the square, sending people shrieking in terror, ducking under wrecked tanks as burning debris rained down on them.

A chorus of cheers rang out from Tranh's unit as the second and third wings of the air assault met the same fate as the first. The C.A.D.S. men still seemed unstoppable. They had parried every blow the Russian high command could muster.

"Only two missiles left," Tranh reported. "Mine." The final squadron made its approach. "Take out the middle two, then try to isolate the others and concentrate SMG fire on them."

Tranh laser-targeted the two craft. Then his twin missiles burst forth, zeroing in on the inner two choppers. The Russian pilots could see the twisted hulks of their comrades' vessels falling onto the Square below them, and broke into evasive tactics early when the rockets first blipped on their radars. But the heat-hungry mini-stingers were on them like white on rice, making widows of Russian women in faraway places.

The two surviving choppers on the flanks broke off their suicidal frontal attack, but a command came over their radios to press forward. It was General Puskinoff, head of the Air Force! "Attack with the N-fives," their commander ordered from afar.

The Russian pilots climbed and moved in, targeting the American positions in the Treasury and the Palace with the new laser weapons. They had never even been tested!

"Hold your ground," Tranh ordered. "We can take these last few guys out with shells; if we compensate for trajectory decay!"

The first ship came in at eye level to the C.A.D.S. commandos. Tranh had positioned himself on a sixth-story balcony of the Palace with two of his men on the rooftop above him and two others on the roof of the Treasury. Between them was a wide chasm where the Square approached the Kremlin walls.

A grand tier of public steps led to the first level of the fortress. Bodies lay strewn about on the ground, and here and there a commando darted about, working his way toward the steps. Tranh ignored them and concentrated on the approaching gunship. They were coming in *close,* strange tubular things extending from their fuselages.

The C.A.D.S. men could see the glint in the eyes of the gunners as they opened up on them. Likewise, the heli-gunners could see the strange nature of the invaders. Exterior-mounted guns on the helis whirred into position and spit armor-piercing shells at the dreaded American blacksuits clinging to the rooftops of the Kremlin. *The lasers were still warming.*

Tranh watched as Marty Lewis, atop the Treasury, was raked across the chest with gunfire, and sent tumbling backward over the roof. Switching to the I.R.-mode, the Oriental could, through dense smoke, see the well-trained trooper fire a grappling hook as he fell, catching himself an anchor and pulling back into position.

"Good work . . ." he radioed.

Preoccupied with the men on the roofs, the chopper crew had completely ignored Tranh, who now opened up on the belly of the aircraft. Holding both firing tubes aloft, he ordered maximum rounds per minute, interspersing an occasional steel dart in the menu for penetration. The concentrated stream of fire bit a hole in the chopper and burned a column of steel through its core. The gunner could feel the floor reverberating below him as the aluminum frame quaked, then buckled, then burst open with raging spikes, chopping his feet and legs into mincemeat. A pool of blood gurgled on his seat and his eyes coasted upward as the chopper arced directly into the public stairs. Too late, the laser-control said, *Ready*. The gunner, as he died, squeezed the trigger. The red laser beam shot out across the Square where it cut swaths across the dead lying there. The stench of searing flesh filled the air.

The final AR-56 pulled up and made a wide circuit of the Kremlin, planning on coming in on the C.A.D.S. force from the west. The chopper's crew could not believe the condition of their capital. Fires raged out of control; the streets were littered with burning cars and trucks; bridges were ruined heaps lying in the middle of rivers. The mad gunners opened fire on the buildings of the Kremlin, shattering banks of windows as they flew by. "Laser now activated," shouted the head gunner. "Come around at coordinates G-seven."

The pilot, a highly decorated veteran of the

Afghani war, dipped his machine over the walls and came screaming in on the balcony where he knew the deadly blacksuits were hiding.

The laser whooped out its straight red line of vaporizing death, slicing the balcony as Tranh's men caught the 'copter in a deadly crossfire. The laser cut one trooper's suit in two and he fell to right and left, burning.

Probability of destruct . . . eighty-nine percent, Tranh read as he instinctively activated his jet-packs and shot up from the balcony as it exploded, hit by another Red-ray so that it burst into a truckload of gravel that crumbled to the pavement eighty feet below.

Tranh hovered in midair and added his firepower to that of his men trained on the chopper as it ran the gamut between them. The C.A.D.S. onslaught proved irresistible as five double-barrel doses of SMGs splintered the airship's plexi-steel windows, sending it down, its pilot slumped over the wheel. It hit, splattering across the Square, spewing glass, steel, and guts in every direction. So much for laser power.

Tranh and his men barely had time to wipe the gunpowder from their visors when they read the second wave of choppers. Twenty-one ice-blue triangles appeared on their screens, each representing a heavily armed transport chopper, cruising sluggishly toward them. Lewis shouted, "Three winged V's of seven ships each, staggered, coming in, lowdown and dirty."

"Here they come boys, ready or not . . ." the Oriental radioed across the band. Sturgis, in the search-building froze in place. The seasoned men knew who Tranh was referring to! Accessing blue-mode they each saw the familiar V-formation on their visor screens; saw the slow, lumbering choppers, straining under the weight of their cargo.

"Graysuits . . ." they each whispered to themselves. "Now the battle begins . . ."

Sturgis was despondent. The graysuits were the equivalent Soviet force—high-tech battle-armored troopers like themselves. Only much, much, more numerous!

CHAPTER 27

Sturgis and his search team hadn't gotten far in their search. They had blasted through ten immense alloy steel shutters before actually reaching the real, inner building.

"Computer . . ." he barked, "ETA of intruder airships . . . give me enemy payload and mark probable attack routes on all visors . . ." He stared at an oil portrait of a glaring Ivan the Terrible while he waited for the response. Finally, the computer readout danced across his screen like a Times Square marquis: *Twenty-one intruder will reach battle zone in two minutes, thirty-three seconds under present conditions . . . Fully armed cargo helicopters carry sixteen air-to-surface antitank rockets each . . . Twin automatic shrapnel guns mounted port and starboard . . . 20-mm AK-30 cannon mounted in nose capable of firing twenty rounds per minute . . .*

The computer next began diagramming probable graysuit attack routes on the C.A.D.S. visors.

Sturgis analyzed each hypothetical situation as it developed. His mind raced with contingencies even as he plunged ahead. He had *decided*. He would continue to lead his commandos and Uzbecs through the Oak Beam Hall, in search of the premier.

"Let's move, men," he ordered, dashing a priceless French armoire down a flight of steps as his men passed him on the run. They moved up the stairs to the maze of wood-paneled corridors and rooms that composed the upper levels of the ancient building. "Trash this place! Shoot anything that moves!"

The Uzbecs took particular joy in the primitive pleasure of vandalism. They ripped Persian carpets and Chinese silks from the walls and wrapped themselves in the finery as they danced from room to room, overturning invaluable antiques, tossing Ming vases through windows, and splattering delicate Dresden porcelain on the floors and walls.

The low-ceilinged, dark building was pretty much devoid of Russians, most everyone having fled through tunnels and passageways to secret exits in the walls of the Kremlin. Here and there, the strike force ran across an old servant still attending his duties, or a drunken, cowering official begging for mercy. There was little mercy to be had from this battle-frenzied crew! They had whipped themselves into a fine frenzy and knew that survival meant maintaining a pitched level of panic throughout the capital.

Shots rang out, executed commies littered the halls, slumped against walls, blood trickling from single holes in their temples. When the powerful fall, they fall hard.

Sturgis, Rossiter, Dixon, and Fireheels led the advance, kicking in door after door, giving a quick look for the premier, then leaving the rooms to the Hunlike depredations of the Uzbecs. Paintings by the masters joined splintered antiques to form crude piles in the middle of rooms which were, in turn, fired by the Uzbecs as they departed. Occasionally, a priceless Fabergé egg lying about on an ambassador's desk would find its way into the pocket of one of the tribesmen. They were vandals—but not fools!

By the time Sturgis and his group had reached the top floor, the building below them was a raging inferno.

"This must be the place," said the colonel as he and Billy came to a broad double door marked Czar's Study in Russian. The two C.A.D.S. men kicked the door down and jumped into the room, their firing tubes on ready. The room was much larger than the others in the building; all in red from the rich carpeting on the floors to the paint on the walls and ceiling. Rows of books filled the cases on the walls and a huge globe filled the center of the room. At the far end, before a tall solitary window, sat a massive desk covered with papers and trinkets, behind which sat a white-haired man.

"Hold your fire, Billy," Sturgis said as his partner prepared to fire. "That's not the premier."

"Comrades!" cried the drunken old-timer behind the desk, standing to meet his guests. "Welcome to Mother Russia!"

He was too drunk to be frightened by the sight of

the huge men clad in black-metal armor. Rather, he simply walked up to each of them, holding a bottle of vodka, and patted each of the U.S. flag medallions on the C.A.D.S. suits. "You cosmonaut-Americans, *nyet?* Welcome! Welcome Americans!"

"Who are you?" Sturgis demanded in broken Russian.

"Oblomov is my name," the servant beamed. "I am the czar ... er ... the premier's tea servant."

"Tea servant!" Billy exclaimed. "What the hell's a tea servant?"

"I serve the czar, er ... *premier* his tea each day." Oblomov carefully removed an ancient timepiece from his vest pocket and gazed at it through bloodshot eyes. "Lessee ..." he stammered in Russian. "By the bones of St. Basil! I'm late!"

"I wouldn't worry about it today," said Sturgis. "I don't think the premier will be taking tea today. By the way, Oblomov, my good man, do you happen to know where we might find the premier right now?"

"Why of course! It is my job to know where the premier is at all times! Do you accuse me of not doing my job?"

"Of course not, Oblomov," Sturgis replied, gazing at the blue blips as they crossed Red Square less than a quarter mile away. "Just tell me where he is. Quick!"

"The premier is taking his steam bath. He should return directly. Would you care to wait for him?" said Oblomov cordially. "I'm sure he would be most glad to meet with friends from across the sea."

"Computer ..." Sturgis ordered, "do you show a location for *steam baths?"*

Working . . . replied the machine. A diagram of the lower Kremlin with a red arrow plotted the course through a tunnel entrance in the yard outside the Oak Beam Hall. It was underground, several levels.

"Do we go after him now?" Fireheels asked.

"Negative," replied Sturgis. "Check your visor. First we deal with the graysuits. Get the Uzbecs and everyone else outside. *Now!*" He couldn't let Tranh's men fight the deadly Russian super-troopers alone, as much as he wanted to find Belyakov.

CHAPTER 28

General Petrin, the commander of the graysuits, was in a 'copter some two miles distant from the conflagration at the Kremlin. He was in his gray-metal armor suit, seated next to Kurchiev, the pilot, scanning the battle with his tech-suit's telescopic-mode. And although he saw many of his AR-56 attack copters go down in flames as they crossed Red Square, he was pleased.

"Kurchiev," Petrin said, "see how the American blacksuits do not fire any more missiles? They have run out of them! Now it is safe for our graysuit force to cable-drop into battle!"

Petrin got on the radio and ordered his wing of twenty-one choppers filled with the Soviet tech-suit force to follow his craft "to victory."

The pilot veered sharply to begin the run, hoping to hell his boss—and friend—Petrin, was right. He usually was. Kurchiev kept low behind an onion dome building. Soon their command heli and its twenty other gunships were crossing over the

Kremlin's decaying stone battlements, taking lots of small-arms fire from the blacksuits stationed along the walls.

"Our shields will stop the bullets," Petrin said confidently. "My God—look! The Presidium, the Golden Palace, and so many other buildings are afire. It appears as if even part of the Oak Beam Hall is afire! Belyakov must be dead, friend Kurchiev. And if that is so, there will be a new premier. Perhaps *me!* But that is for later. Right now, the American raiders must be destroyed."

"Yes," Kurchiev agreed, wheeling about and hovering. "And there is only a handful of them, while we have a hundred graysuits!" The sophisticated scanners on their craft showed the enemy deployment in much the same manner as blue-mode.

Petrin swung the chopper's door open and pressed the button on a winch. A heavy metal arm moved out the side of the aircraft and started spewing out a long steel cable. Petrin locked his metal hand grips on it and swung out, beginning his slide down the cable. "Wish us luck, Kurchiev!"

All around the Kremlin grounds, each of the twenty other choppers were disgorging their compliments of five metal-suited soldiers each. The odds were ten to one in the Soviets' favor.

Petrin hit the ground easily and let go of the cable. Then he ordered the other graysuits to descend and advance upon the pockets of Amercians. "Use your rocket-grenades, not bullets, comrades."

The Soviets spread out under sporatic fire as they landed. Two men were hit with some sort of explosive shell and blew apart into aluminum foil and meltstones. Petrin ordered, "Blast the hell out of the Amercians, be brave."

Petrin was no fool. He knew that Colonel Sturgis was undoubtedly leading this attack. Only such a genius could have penetrated the Kremlin itself and wasted two-thirds of it! Petrin was also well aware that Sturgis's blacksuit corps had bested his own elite force many times.* But now, Petrin thought proudly, he had better men and better armored graysuits! There would be victory this time.

Petrin ducked behind the monumental base of a statue of some previous party secretary and scanned the spread-out Americans with his sensors, trying to pick up their radio transmissions. He knew the battle's outcome would depend entirely on killing the American Caesar, Col. Dean Sturgis.

From their various positions around the burning Kremlin, the C.A.D.S. men watched in hardened horror as the sky darkened with transports dispatching dozens of mechanized commandos descending upon them on winched cables. Gray steel boots clanked on the cobblestone as the Russians touched down. The chilling clink of activated weapon systems rippled through the enclosed streets and alleyways of the capital.

Billy, characteristically, was the first to draw blood in the renewed combat. As the Russian elite fell from the sky, he took careful aim and, with a single SMG shot, clipped the metal cable supporting one graysuit as he descended.

* See C.A.D.S. #3.

227

The two-hundred-foot, headfirst fall shorted out the Russian's computer and activated his firing mechanisms. A hail of rocket fire erupted skyward through his upstretched weapon-tubes. The crowd of choppers overhead scurried to escape this unexpected attack from their own man. The jumbo 'copters managed to evade the errant shots, but two of them crossed tails and, tail rotor blades smashed, they spun out of control, crashing spectacularly amid the spires of a cathedral just outside the Kremlin walls.

Meanwhile, the fallen graysuit flipped about on the pavement like a fish on a dock, a captive in his robot-shell-gone-mad. When the complex cooling system gave out, the main flaw in the Soviet graysuit design was that his power packs overheated and green servo-gas—poisonous gasses—quickly filled the suit, snuffing out the life of its occupant.

Billy had managed to eliminate two choppers and a graysuit with a single bullet.

"Good work," said Sturgis, standing with Fireheels and the rest of his men outside the burning timbers of the hallowed Oak Beam Hall. Still there was plenty of work to do as the courtyard before them was suddenly lousy with graysuits.

"Here comes Tranh, Skip," said Billy.

Sturgis, pondering the dimensions of his problems, turned to see Tranh rounding a corner at the helm of a huge motorcycle with a sidecar holding two of his men. Immediately behind him another of his men drove a similar cycle. The two big bikes roared up to Sturgis and his men, huddled among the silenced tanks that Fireheels and his men had taken out earlier. A light bulb clicked in Sturgis's mind.

"You men," he said, pointing to the C.A.D.S. warriors in the sidecars, "get in those tanks and get ready to open fire on the Square."

Then the colonel got into the seat of one of the bikes alongside of Tranh. "C'mon Billy," he said. "Climb aboard. Fireheels, you join Tranh."

The men jumped into the sidecars. "Good," said Sturgis. "Now, hand each other your cable hook-ups."

"What?" said Billy.

"Don't ask questions!" said Sturgis, revving his engine and slipping the hog into first. "Tranh, you get the idea?"

"Round up time at the OK corral?" asked Tranh.

"You got it, buddy," replied Sturgis with a smile.

While several of the C.A.D.S. men hauled the dead Russian bodies out of the tanks and took up their positions, Sturgis and Tranh roared forward, out from the alleyways behind the buildings on the east end of the Kremlin into the open courtyard where the graysuits had accumulated.

"Open fire!" shouted Petrin to his men from behind the statue where he was directing operations. "It's the Americans!"

The Russian mechanoids reacted too slowly as the C.A.D.S. troopers careened like buzz bombs around the yard, dodging this way and that amid sizzling rockets that skipped past them and stinging bullets that bounced off their protective suits. As the

Americans neared their prey, they broke off. The double metal cable suspended between the cycles was fed out by Billy and Fireheels. When they were about a hundred yards apart, Sturgis and Tranh began a circling movement, entangling two dozen of the graysuits in their iron web. Those graysuits who managed to escape the trap tried firing on the C.A.D.S. men, only to see their shots absorbed by their own comrades. The motorcycle pilots tightened the noose, circling tighter and tighter, while their passengers winched their cables ever more powerfully, trussing the commies up like a Thanksgiving turkey ready for the roaster. Then the men in the tanks, rolling from an alley, opened fire on the captive audience.

The trapped graysuits were helpless, their weapons-tubes strapped to their sides. When they tried to jet-pack up, they created even more destruction among their ranks. The heat and strain caused several of the graysuits to overheat and discharge their weapons, hitting comrades point-blank with armor-shattering blows.

Petrin was aghast. His crack unit was being decimated before his eyes at the first shock of combat.

"Idiots! Cowards!" he screamed through his radio as he watched the metal motorcyclists wrap up his men in a nice Christmas bundle while other Americans trained the powerful barrels of Soviet tanks on the grays, ripping wide gaps in their ranks, enfilading them with blockbuster armor-piercing cannon shells.

After sealing the bulk of the unit in a puffing,

belching Gordian knot of hyper-stagnation, Sturgis and Tranh broke free, running wild around the courtyard picking off strays with their V.S.F.'s shells. Billy stood in the sidecar and howled, whipping a steel cable into a lasso and snagging one of the grayusuits by the neck.

"Get along little doggy!" he wailed. "I ain't had so much fun since I won the Oklahoma State Bronco Bustin' champeenship back in eighty-seven." The crazy-for-killing Southerner gunned his smoke-pony and sped down an alleyway, dragging the graysuit behind him. Billy gave his cable a twist and sent the tin-can commie rolling to the Uzbecs who had armed themselves with antitank launchers culled from the death grip of Soviet soldiers. Zandark stood twenty feet from the graysuit as it rolled to a stop at his feet and pounded a three-pound shell into his visor.

"Bring more!" the excited Uzbec chief called.

"You got it!" answered Billy as he and Sturgis sped back out to the square for another gray, who had panicked.

Tranh and Fireheels proved no less effective. Using his jet-pack to effect a tackle, the powerful Indian simply wrestled his prey to the ground from behind and wrapped a powerful headlock across his visor screen, squeezing with servo-augumented steel arms until he shattered the plate and crushed his victim's face. One bulky Russian, however, proved equal to Fireheels's challenge.

"Ah," said Petrin, when he saw the American jump to the back of his man, Boris Bukolik, "now the Yankee has met his match. Surely Boris will

231

vindicate us!"

The Russian, an Olympic gold medalist in both power-lifting and wrestling, felt the impact on his back and immediately threw Fireheels over his hip, sending the Indian flying across the yard, bending a lamppost and crashing into a jeep. Fireheels disappeared behind the wreck with Bukolik in hot pursuit.

"I will tear you to pieces with my hands!" screamed the mad Russian.

Sturgis sped to the center of the Square to help Fireheels, but a gray, seeing the colonel's move, raked his cycle with two RPGs, shattering the wheel assemblies and sending Sturgis and Billy tumbling across the cobblestones.

"He's got Fireheels!" shouted Billy as the two men righted themselves. Sturgis could see the big Russian reach into the smoke behind the burning jeep and hoist Fireheels above his head. Then, the Indian's suit exploded, taking the Russian with it.

"Fireheels!" cried Billy.

"No!" yelled Sturgis. "Look!" He pointed to a nearby lamppost, behind which lurked the wily native, waving a metal salute.

"He threw a *gray* at him," laughed Billy.

"And then fired a one-oh-five shell," said Sturgis. Tranh pulled up on his cycle and picked up Fireheels, speeding the Indian—invulnerable man out of harm's way. A Red's shell smashed a crater where Fireheels had just stood!

Sturgis scanned the square, searching for the man who had shot the bike out from under Billy and him. He picked up a blip behind a big marble statue to the

232

left. He tele-zoomed in visually, saw the stars on the helmet. "It has to be Petrin," he breathed. "That sly fox is laying for me . . ."

"Move out," the colonel ordered Billy, motioning his man to cover him on the right. Sturgis wanted Petrin himself. He moved to the opposite side of the base of the statue. The two tech-commandos stood back-to-back on opposite sides of the stone megalith, twenty feet apart, staring at each others blip on their screen. Was Petrin's scanners picking him up?

Sturgis sprang like a cat, capitalizing on Petrin's hesitation. He jetted to the top of the stone base, which supported a huge bronze statue of Khrushchev holding a globe. Digging his metal fingers under the ten-ton statue, he summoned his servo-driven strength and popped its supporting bolts, then threw his shoulder into it, toppling the figure enough to send it tumbling over the side.

Petrin fired feverishly at nothing as the brass bullshitter hit him from nowhere, pinning him, severing his right arm completely.

Sturgis peered over the edge of the base. Petrin lay in a pool of blood, his suit smoldering with shorts. "Dying," said Sturgis, "or dead." A series of titanic explosions behind lit up the sky. He wouldn't have time to check. So far the C.A.D.S. force had been lucky, and they had helped themselves by sticking to a rigid schedule and maintaining panic among the Russians. Now, they were low on ammo, their suits were at minimal power, and the men were near exhaustion. Hours of intense combat in the cumbersome suits was taking its toll.

"Let's get the hell out of here—back through the

tunnels," Billy yelled. "The graysuits are with-drawing."

Sturgis wanted to do just that, and to rejoin Robin. But he knew he must press on. He knew he had a higher duty.

"No," Sturgis objected. "We must kill Belyakov. We must go down to the steam baths. He could still be there, hiding."

CHAPTER 29

Sturgis and Billy Dixon plunged down the staircase leading to the premier's private steam baths far below ground. The spiral stone stairs descended down, down, until they were in a catacomb that looked like it might have been there in Ivan the Terrible's time—and had been!

The vaulted stone ceiling had some modern fluorescent lights though, and the place was clean. The C.A.D.S. men were unchallenged as they strode down the flagstone flooring, following some arrows painted on the wall. They passed a power-dead bank of elevators.

Soon Sturgis saw steam in the air. "The water must be from the Moskva River," he said. "We're below it here, Billy. This side of the Kremlin's walls reach right underneath it."

"Place gives me the creeps!" Billy responded. "But it's warm. My suit's temp guage says it's up to eighty-six degrees! Pretty wild, for Russia in the winter, right Skip?"

"Shhh!" Sturgis exclaimed. His ampli-mode had

picked up talking—nearby. The colonel heard: ". . . Premier Belyakov. The last reports were that Petrin's graysuits had arrived and were mopping up the last few intruders."

Sturgis's computer indicated the person speaking was a hundred and fifty feet dead ahead in the hot mists.

A second talker began. "Sergei, that makes no sense at all! Why, if the graysuits are winning upstairs, have we lost communications?"

"P-perhaps the fighting cut a telephone line, premier! Shall I go up and—"

"No! Stay here with me! Just keep trying to raise Glassnose. Damn! I knew I should have had Petrin's men, not Glassnose's division, as guards. This should never have happened! Sergei, if Glassnose survives this, remind me to have him shot."

Sturgis smiled. Ahead were three men: two guards, and possibly the premier himself. He activated the SMG system on his weapon choice. He wouldn't kill a double; there were safeguards for that. Motioning Billy to follow him, he moved forward as noiselessly as possible in the armor. About fifty feet further into the steam, Sturgis heard a sharp intake of breath, then the words, "Who is there? Identify yourselves!"

Sturgis, in his best Russian, replied on his suit-speaker. "It is Glassnose! I have an important prisoner for interrogation by the premier himself. Come and give me a hand with this American dog!"

The two guards conferred in whispers. They were suspicious, but still they came forward. Both soon appeared on I.R.-mode. Sturgis didn't fire—yet. He wanted to knock them out—silently. But they both lifted guns when they saw Sturgis.

The colonel wanted as little noise as possible, so he fired the quiet way—a pair of six-inch darts, poisoned with an instant-death drug. A Van Patten specialty for the chief assassin. The noise was just a *phoot, phoot,* but it echoed alarmingly in the steamy corridor.

As the darts hurtled forward, for an instant Sturgis caught the horrified look in one soldier's eye. He tried to jump aside but didn't have a chance. The dart pinned him to the birch-panel walls.

Sturgis and Billy strode forward, stepping over the two uniformed men. Their metal suits were dripping with condensation from the heat, their visors partly fogged. It was surreal. In waves of color, the lone man ahead was outlined in the C.A.D.S. visor's I.D. Probe grid lines. Sturgis watched the computer superimpose a whole series of photos of the premier from its files onto the man's image. The readout confirmed: *Subject in view identified as Soviet Premier Yuri A. Belyakov. Subject not a look-alike.*

The premier, in a worried tone, said, "Sergei? Sasha? What was that odd noise? Is someone there? Is it Glassnose? Glassnose? Is that you?"

"I.R.-mode," Sturgis said. The premier's super-heated body lit up on the colonel's visor screen like a red flare. Sturgis could see he was naked, sitting with just a blue towel around his waist, thirty feet ahead. Sturgis and Billy just walked up to him.

To the premier, the visitation by the twin black-metal men was like a nightmare on the grandest scale! He could barely see them—horrific things half lost in the mist. And another fright: He felt his feet wet—and when he looked down, he saw a stream of blood had come down the slanting corridor and was pooling at his toes.

"Sergei? P-please . . . it is a graysuit?"

No answer.

He backed off, but where was there to go? Only to the heated granite wall. The warm air was now a stifling, smothering pillow.

"W—who are you? Are you—graysuits?"

Silence.

No, not silence. The metallic creaking of the metal men approaching. The premier strained his eyes and saw a single eye glowing in the dim light; antennas—like an ant. *"Robots!"*

"No, we're not robots, Premier Belyakov. The opposite—*Americans!*"

"Sergei!" the premier screamed. "Sasha! Come at once!"

"Don't bother to call for your guards. They're dead," Sturgis intoned dryly.

The premier stood up straight and inhaled, trying to get a hold of himself. He managed to calm himself a bit, resign himself. No one lives forever. This was his time to die. Why die a coward? He said, "Very good—you have defeated all my forces, I assume. Now you come here to kill me."

Sturgis said, "Yes."

"Very, very *good!* I wish I had commandos like you two! That you could do such a thing—penetrate the Kremlin and find me! Brilliant, and very brave!"

*   *   *

Sturgis had not been prepared for this. Belyakov was obviously resigned to his fate. Sturgis had hoped—expected—that he would confront a sniveling coward, someone he would enjoy killing. No one enjoyed killing a brave man.

"Mind if I get a robe?" the premier asked.

"Do it very slowly," Sturgis nodded. The colonel watched the premier go to a hook and pick up a maroon robe and put it on.

"Before you kill me—who are you?"

"The name's Dean Sturgis. And this is Billy. U.S. Special C.A.D.S. Forces."

"Indeed? Well that's remarkable—remarkable. I commend you. Now do your duty—kill me!" He bared his flabby chest. There was just the slightest quiver in his fleshy lips as Sturgis lifted his weapon-tube arm and heard the load-click. But the colonel hesitated. "Before you die, answer one question," Sturgis asked. "The question is . . . Why?"

"Why what? Oh, I see—why did I launch my nuclear strike against America? Why did I destroy the United States?"

"Yes. Why did you do it? Why risk your people; the world's ecosystem?"

"Because my friend, war was inevitable—when the INF agreement and Start nuclear missile treaties between our nations were not followed up; when your Zenith Star anit-ballistic missile space laser satellites were launched ahead of ours, I knew that the U.S. would sooner or later attack us! So I attacked first."

"But no one could win a nuclear war—didn't you understand that?" Sturgis objected.

The premier sighed. "Our experts, General Veloshnikov, *everyone* assured me that you would not have the power to overcome our secret laser defense shield. They said that we Soviets would not lose a single city. But we did, alas. We lost many!"*

"But surely you knew that the fallout would have blown over your nation, even if you weren't hit. The Chernobyl accident in 1986 should have made you realize how far even *one* explosion's fallout cloud spreads."

"We had calculated a tenfold increase in radiation worldwide—acceptable for a final solution to the conflicts between our nations. Do you want me to say I'm sorry? Well I *am* sorry!" The premier wiped his trembling hands through his thinning hair. "So shoot me. Go ahead—you'll be doing me a favor."

There were running noises down the steamy corridor now. The C.A.D.S. men had just a few seconds at best. But Sturgis had never shot a defenseless, naked man before and he hesitated to do so.

Billy pushed him aside. "If you don't want to do it, Skip, I'll gladly waste this turd!" The Southerner lifted his kill-arm and fired a full clip of explosive bullets into the premier, severing the man's torso, splattering the wall crimson.

"Come on, Skip, we did our job. Now let's get out of here."

Sturgis looked down for a second at the bullet-butchered corpse of a man who, seconds before, had been the ruler of the world. Then he followed Dixon up the corridor.

* See C.A.D.S.—the first book.

CHAPTER 30

In the deepest recesses of the Kremlin's sub-basement "trysting rooms," General Dzelosky had just mounted the beautiful, firm naked body of the Bolshoi's lead ballerina when the phone rang. And it did not stop ringing. The noise won out over his erection and the general cursed and reached over to the receiver, picking it up. "Yes? What is it? It better be g—"

"Sir! This is Lieutenant Merskov! They are attacking all over the Kremlin."

"Who? Who is attacking? Get a hold of yourself, man."

"We . . . we think it is C.A.D.S. troopers, U.S. commandos, sir! They have black-metal suits. They—they've mowed down most of the Politboro members already. And the Presidium is afire. The whole place is ablaze."

"And Belyakov," Dzelosky shouted, "what of the premier? Is he alive?"

"That's it, sir—we think he was in the steam baths.

Some of the Americans went down into there after him. I can't raise Sergei, none of the premier's guards! No one is in command anymore. Glassnose was leading the counterattack near the Presidium and he was killed. Major Strelski died along the walls! Shall I send our shock divisions down to try and rescue the premier?"

Gears were turning in Dzelosky's rusty brain now. Gears that stopped his inner vision on a pleasant picture. *Premier Dzelosky. Yes!* The whole Politburo was dead. Premier Belyakov was dead. So why not a strong, handsome and *virile* general as the new premier?

"No, don't send any help to Belyakov. Don't do anything. I'll be right up. Is the number five exit open and safe?"

"Yes sir. We have twenty men covering it."

"Good. I'll be right up." He put the phone down. "Sorry, Irena. But when I come back, I shall be premier, not just a general!"

When Dzelosky reached the surface, he had decided on which order he would give. "Have your men open the main floodgates to the Moskva River, Lieutenant Merskov! Flood all the areas below ground to destroy the invaders."

"But sir . . . the steam baths are on the lowest level! The premier will be killed!"

"He is not a concern now. Do what I say, fool!"

The lieutenant caught the glint in Dzelosky's eye and understood. If the general was to become premier by drowning the old premier, then he, a mere lieutenant now, might also expect a promotion. A slight smirk was on the lieutenant's lips as he said, "I will open all the valves to the Moskva River immediately! We must drown the invaders!"

As rockets screamed overhead and small-arms fire flew every which way, Dzelosky said, "You are good, lieutenant. I shall remember this completely when the time comes. When I am premier, Lieutenant Merskov, you and I shall have a drink."

"Most definitely, *Premier* Dzelosky!"

But things were not to be so simple as that. As word spread of the deaths of the Politburo members—and most likely the death of the premier— several other high-ranking generals had like thoughts of ultimate power. And as word spread all over Russia, Soviet units were turning their guns on one another.

Indeed, it seemed that everyone wanted to seize the reigns of power. But none of these pip-squeaks was to be successful.

Eight thousand one hundred miles to the west, and twenty-five thousand, six-hundred and thirty feet down, on the bottom of the icy North Atlantic, Supreme Marshal Veloshnikov sat in quiet contemplation. The man was dressed in an immaculately tailored black high-collared uniform. He stood in the cool circular observation room called the Nautilus Room, at the nose of his three-hundred-meter-long nuclear submarine command center, *The Lenin.*

For days now, the command-submarine had been lying still and silent like a sleeping devil fish as Veloshnikov studied the KGB-gathered folders before him. He had been obsessed with the deteriorating political situation in the Soviet world empire. There were strange events, secretive moves, unseen alliances. A dozen forces were vying for control of the Kremlin, vying against his beloved Premier Belyakov. Only waiting for a chance.

Veloshnikov had decided on a course of action. He would recommend to the premier the expulsion—and death—of three high-ranking traitors:

1) Maj. Yuri Danirov of the Arkansas sector of Occupied America. Danirov was a young upstart, and had failed to report an encounter with the American commando leader, Colonel Sturgis. He could be up to no good and was charismatic.

2) General Petrin of the graysuits unit. Petrin had never made a move against the premier—or Veloshnikov. But he was *too good.* Men would follow him if he decided to attempt a coup. He had to go.

3) Adm. Sergei Danlovitch, head of the Pacific Submarine Fleet. He was far from the homeland, often going ashore in the low-radioactivity Pacific Peace Zone's Neutral Islands. KGB HQ reported that Danlovitch had been exposed to tainted nonsocialist ideas.

Veloshnikov put the hit list down. His self-imposed days of silence, of noncommunication with the outside world, was over. It had done wonders for his analytical abilities. He was sure, with these three traitors out of the way, another decade would pass before he, supreme leader of the armed forces, or the premier, would ever be challenged.

Veloshnikov leaned back and looked out through the wide rectangular magna-glass porthole. The undersea world was an ever shifting panorama of strangeness. Right now, *The Lenin's* floodlight illuminated a school of strange-glowing squid. He watched them slowly drift past the lights in the murky water. Life was so amazing; even down here at hundreds of pounds per square inch of pressure there were creatures, living creatures. Life was pervasive, enduring, resilient. If a billion surface-dwelling humans had died in the Nuke War, so be it! Perhaps another billion creatures had been born down here to compensate. He smiled—perhaps in a few weeks, when the three suspected traitors meet their death, they would be reincarnated down here, as squid, or sucker fish—and Veloshnikov would see them slide past this window.

There was a knock on the door.

"I am not to be disturbed," he snarled.

"Sir—I know what you said." It was Assistant Duty Officer Roganov's squealy voice. "But there is an extreme situation that has arisen."

"Come in then. It better be important."

The pale, trembling young officer entered, carrying a red KGB dispatch. "This just came," Roganov said, holding out the dispatch.

"Impossible. All communication was cut off by my orders!"

"Overridden sir, by the KGB command in Moscow. They turned our communication systems back on and fed this urgent telex through."

Veloshnikov felt sick. Could they do that? He hadn't known the KGB had such technical power! Trembling, he took the thin film of paper into his hands, and read:

Kremlin under attack since 0900 hours. Premier Belyakov believed dead. Entire Politburo dead. Raiders are American blacksuit commando team, number uncertain. Means of arrival uncertain. Blacksuits believed to be withdrawing, but fighting still rages. Three separate factions of our own forces now vying for control of the government. Advise with urgent speed on your decision to counter threat. We recognize you as next in line for premier's post.

KGB SUPREME HQ
Major Devisk

Veloshnikov crushed the paper in his hand and slammed his fist down on the table. "Roganov, take my reply to Major Devisk at once. Here, send this reply." Veloshikov scribbled out: My orders are for your KGB forces to support whatever faction of traitors appears to be losing battle for control of our beloved government. Keep any side from ascendancy. I am on my way. Veloshnikov.

He handed the note to Roganov. "Deliver this to the radio room."

The young officer saluted and turned to convey

the orders. As soon as Roganov was out the door, Veloshnikov got on the intercom and said, "This is the supreme marshal. I order all systems powered up. We are leaving the ocean floor. We set sail immediately at full speed for Archangel Harbor."

As Veloshnikov gathered his papers and shoved them in a leather attache case, he heard the squawking buzzer sounding general quarters go off, and then he felt the floor beneath him shift. As he turned to leave the Nautilus Room, the metal shields outside the port window were closing—a combat-speed precaution. He had to stagger against the steep incline of the red-carpeted hall outside, holding onto the grips on the railings, to keep on his feet. A dozen crewmen and women rushed past him rallying to their tasks, barely acknowledging his presence.

Veloshnikov found his way through the bedlam, took the B elevator—a sickening sideway-and-up ride—to the command room. He opened its door and came into the dim red-lit cabin filled with computer screens and instruments. The two drivers were sitting at their controls. A massive number of readouts were pouring over the screens arrayed before them. The marshal looked at the depth guage. It was spinning almost too fast to be seen—depth twenty-three thousand . . . twenty-two thousand . . . twenty-one thousand . . .

He moved up toward his command seat. Gripping the backrest of the floor-attached chair, he sat down and strapped in. There were creakings and snappings in the metal walls all around them as the pressure let up on the heavy plates as they rose in the ocean. A low roar from the five nuclear engines propelling them up to cruising depth of two thousand feet made him shout when he asked, "Status?"

"Speed, thirty-five knots, bearing north, northeast!" someone called out.

"Never mind statistics! When do we get to Russia!" Veloshnikov demanded.

The same voice that had been calling out the bearing replied, "Two days, sir."

Veloshnikov buried his head in his hands. "Too *long. Too long,*" he muttered. He tried to get a hold of himself. There must be some way of getting there faster. Some way—*yes!*

"What is our closest land mass?"

"Iceland, sir." Again it was Roganov. "We can be in Reykjavik in ten hours."

"Iceland?" Veloshnikov smiled. There was an airbase there—and there would be an SST. He could be in Moscow in thirteen hours. That was better—enough time to rally his forces, and the KGB's men; and make sure that he, the legitimate heir to power, and not some upstart, became the new premier.

"Reset course for Iceland," he ordered. "Quickly!"

CHAPTER 31

The two C.A.D.S. troopers, leaving the premier sprawled in his own blood, gunned down a pack of soldiers in the steamy tunnel. Confronted by a sudden cave-in caused by a Soviet charge, unable to reach the stairs, they took another route. It was evident they were heading up, and that was good.

They were soon on the second level—the one where Robin's cell had been, when they heard a roar. Billy was the first to understand what it was: rushing water.

"Skip, they're flooding the tunnels," he gasped. "We've got to get out of here—to the surface. Forget the tunnel to the tomb! Our suits will short out!"

"Yeah," Sturgis replied grimly. "Computer-analyze direction of water source."

Computing . . . Twenty-three degrees west . . . Also lesser amount one hundred twenty degrees west.

Sturgis and his companion reached a corner in the tunnels. "Head down this east tunnel, Billy. We'll get to the surface, I promise you. Then to the tomb via terra firma."

They continued their mad flight, but all the time they had been running, the damned P.O.D. (probability of destruction index) rose. Soon they were wading, not running. *P.O.D. eighty-nine.*

"Skip! This corridor—it's a dead end!"

"Yeah, the map is wrong, or they built a wall here since it was made." The colonel was up against solid rock.

"What do we do?"

"The P.O.D. hit *ninety-nine.*

"Something—anything. Fire explosive .105 mm shells together. Try to blow the wall. Step back!"

The water was up to their waists now. Sturgis raised his sleeve and fired. So did Billy. The explosive shells flashed out and hit the wall, caving in a pile of bricks. The C.A.D.S. troopers climbed over the rubble and into a drier corridor. They continued onward.

A roaring. "Shit Skip, there's a tidal wave coming at us from the other end!"

"Computer," Sturgis snapped out, "probe density of adjacent walls and ceiling!"

"Look—see that steel plating? Must be a repair job on the ceiling. Use your bare metal hands, Billy. We have the strength of twenty men."

Using their steel fingers like puncture tools to grab hold of the metal and then like pliers to pry it, they dug with all their might up through solid metal, dropping the debris below, into the water.

Sturgis's fingers hurt like they'd never hurt before,

and his servo-assists were kicking out one by one.

"The suit is beginning to fight me," Billy exclaimed. "My leg-servos have cut out—my suit's legs are dead! I don't think I can go on—leave me behind, Skip."

"Never." They were neck deep.

Then Sturgis heard a *whoosh* and saw a patch of daylight.

"We've got through!"

And just in time; for behind them came welling up all the accumulated pressure of a billion gallons of cold river water! Like two corks in champagne bottles the troopers exploded up in a veritable geyser. They were propelled thirty feet into the air, used their jets to land on their feet. "You okay?"

"Okay—now to get out of the Kremlin!" said Billy. They were already taking incoming fire from every quarter. Billy froze in place.

"Billy—can you move?"

"I don't—*yes!* The servos cut in again—I can run!"

"Then do it man, *do it!*"

Shells hit the ground twenty feet away. They commenced to zigzag run, guided on their erratic jags by the computer analysis of shell trajectories. They were at the wall.

"Use grapple darts and cables . . . we'll climb down—jet-pack systems are down!"

"Right Skip."

"Fire them!"

The grapple projectiles slammed into the wall, dug in, then opened inside the brick, like claws. The

251

attached cables were capable of holding a grand piano—or something equally weighty—a C.A.D.S. commando!

First Sturgis and then his companion dropped down over the wall like black-metal spiders. Twenty seconds later the colonel and Billy hit the ground and detached from the cable, making toward their headquarters in the field, Lenin's tomb.

EPILOGUE

There was much to do and much to say and no time for any of it in the crypt of the father of communism. Outside, thundering hordes mustered with savage intensity. Only now had the full dimension of the attack become a reality to the Russians, *all* Russians: politicians, military men, and private citizens. All of Moscow clustered about the glowing embers of their sacred epicenter. The glow of the fires danced on their ashen faces, reflected in their unbelieving eyes.

Sturgis grabbed Amarr. "Where's Robin!"

"G-guards' room. Safe and well."

Sturgis removed the helmet from his suit and rushed toward it. He noticed, as he pushed through the happy celebrants of victory, that the Uzbecs clustered in a corner, jabbering and staring at an array of baubles they had stolen. Zandark was already spouting an epic poem of his deeds. The colonel opened the door.

Sturgis smiled as Robin chirped his name from

across the room and flew into his arms, embracing him just like in the pictures. They were alone only for a moment.

"Er . . . excuse me, colonel," Fenton said, after a pause of courtesy. "Would the colonel care to initiate a rapid withdrawal at this point?"

"If you mean do I want to get the fuck out of here, you're *damned right!*" growled Sturgis. "Any trucks left?"

"We managed to hang onto all of them intact," replied Carson, one of the men who had remained guarding the tomb-base. "It's right outside the door."

"Good work. Get the stuff loaded in. Billy, take the first wheel. Wosyck, Fenton take the other two trucks. Everyone back in trucker outfits! Shove the C.A.D.S. stuff in back! Zandark! Go get your men in the trucks. And keep quiet! Tranh, we ride out of town nice and easy . . . like we owned the place. I think that's our only chance."

"Got it, Skip. But I doubt—"

"No doubts!"

The pack of raiders trundled into the Russian trucks in the shadows of heavy smoke. Within a hundred yards, company after company of Red Guards and Soviet regulars formed up into columns, preparing to enter the Kremlin, unaware the battle was no longer there!

"You there! In that truck!" yelled a snappy Russian lieutenant marshaling his squadron into line. The C.A.D.S. men, in their khaki trucker

254

parkas, continued to board the trucks.

Wosyck pointed his finger innocently at himself, as if to say, "me?" Sturgis hustled Robin, bundled in a parka, into Wosyck's truck. He kept his fingers on a pistol.

"You! Yes, you!" the lieutenant shouted. "Get those trucks the hell out of here! You're blocking our advance! Do you hear me?"

The rest of the C.A.D.S. men and Uzbecs got in the trucks rapidly, amused looks on their faces.

Wosyck smiled and saluted, gunned the engine, shifted into first, and jumped into motion, heading east across Red Square through the city streets, followed by Fenton and Billy's trucks.

The C.A.D.S. force, together with their band of Uzbec tribesmen, had just wasted the Kremlin. Behind them, every major building within that citadel lay engulfed in ruin. The core of the Russian political machine had been executed, and the Russian Empire was in a state of utter chaos!

The Americans had indeed stung. As their truck rolled through the hills and valleys on the outskirts of Moscow, every member of the attack force felt sorrow over the loss of several close friends—and deep pride in their achievement! For the first time, they had taken the fight to the Russians. And they had won!

ASHES
by William W. Johnstone

OUT OF THE ASHES (1137, $3.50)

Ben Raines hadn't looked forward to the War, but he knew it was coming. After the balloons went up, Ben was one of the survivors, fighting his way across the country, searching for his family, and leading a band of new pioneers attempting to bring American OUT OF THE ASHES.

FIRE IN THE ASHES (1310, $3.50)

It's 1999 and the world as we know it no longer exists. Ben Raines, leader of the Resistance, must regroup his rebels and prep them for bloody guerrilla war. But are they ready to face an even fiercer foe — the human mutants threatening to overpower the world!

ANARCHY IN THE ASHES (1387, $3.50)

Out of the smoldering nuclear wreckage of World War III, Ben Raines has emerged as the strong leader the Resistance needs. When Sam Hartline, the mercenary, joins forces with an invading army of Russians, Ben and his people raise a bloody banner of defiance to defend earth's last bastion of freedom.

SMOKE FROM THE ASHES (2191, $3.50)

Swarming across America's Southern tier march the avenging soldiers of Libyan blood terrorist Khamsin. Lurking in the blackened ruins of once-great cities are the mutant Night People, crazed killers of all who dare enter their domain. Only Ben Raines, his son Buddy, and a handful of Ben's Rebel Army remain to strike a blow for the survival of America and the future of the free world!

ALONE IN THE ASHES (1721, $3.50)

In this hellish new world there are human animals and Ben Raines — famed soldier and survival expert — soon becomes their hunted prey. He desperately tries to stay one step ahead of death, but no one can survive ALONE IN THE ASHES.